Jay studied Nora with cold, measuring eyes.

"Up until about now I thought anything that concerned you concerned me, too, because I had the idiotic notion that I was in love with you. That's pretty silly, isn't it?"

"It certainly is!" Nora snapped hotly. "I can't think of anything sillier."

Jay stood quite still for a moment, and then he lifted his hands, palm upward, in a gesture that marked his defeat.

"That being the case, then it's also pretty ridiculous for me to try to stop you making a fool of yourself over your pretty gigolo, isn't it? I'm sure if you'll hurry back to your rendezvous you'll find him still waiting."

Nora was fighting against the angry tears that threatened her.

Belmont Books is proud to announce a completely new series of novels published as Belmont Romance Books. These novels, written by top-flight authors, tell of the heartbreaks, complications—and beauty—of enduring love. For a complete listing see back pages of this book.

Wedding Song

A love story by Peggy Gaddis

The Complete Edition

BELMONT BOOKS   •   NEW YORK CITY

About the Author

PEGGY GADDIS is perhaps the most popular and prolific writer of novels for women. She is the author of more than 300 published novels and is best known for her nurse and romantic fiction. Miss Gaddis has been editor of Motion Picture Magazine, and served as staff writer for Dell Publications and several newspapers. She began her career as a screenwriter. She is the author of several bestselling novels in the Belmont Romance Series.

1

NORA LEFT the bus at the corner and walked half a block back along the street to the wrought-iron fence with a low gate that enclosed the Robinson property. Her pretty mouth was a thin line of weariness as she looked at the big, stately old house that was set back at the end of the broken cement walk.

Because it was crowded by a smart new apartment building that towered eight stories high on one side, and by an office building that was twelve stories high on the other, the gray stone house dwelt continually in shadow that made it seem even drearier than it should have. The ancient boxwoods along the walk were badly in need of trimming; the evergreen shrubbery that surrounded the house had grown to the point where it seemed to peer inquisitively through the long windows.

Nora sighed as she swung open the gate and plodded along the walk to the big front door with its impressive fan-light. She paused, as she rummaged in her bag for her key.

The door behind Nora opened and she turned, startled, to see the elderly maid, Mattie, standing there eyeing her coldly.

"I thought maybe you'd forgot your key, miss, the way your mother always does," Mattie said curtly as she stood aside to let Nora enter.

"I was just standing there, Mattie, thinking of all the changes this old place has seen in its lifetime," Nora said.

"I guess it's seen its share, Miss Nora," Mattie admitted, and her tone warmed a bit. "Shame you and your mother can't sell it and go live in a nice apartment."

"I know, Mattie, but Mother won't even discuss selling."

"But your father left you as executor of the estate, miss." She broke off as Nora's expression chilled slightly, and said brusquely, "Well, everybody knows that, miss. Would you like some tea?"

"If you don't mind, Mattie—" Nora's face burned with shame as she heard a note of apology in her voice.

"Well, why should I, miss? My wages have been paid up until tomorrow, when I'm leaving. Might as well do what I can for you long as I'm here," said Mattie, and stumped stolidly out of the room.

Nora's lips curled slightly.

With well-trained servants so scarce, and the demand so terrific, small wonder all the Robinson staff had been able to step straight from the Robinson service into even better paid jobs. Mattie was the last to leave. Tomorrow she would be gone, and Nora and Celia, her mother, would be alone in the big, stately old house.

Mattie came back with a tea tray and deposited it on a low table. Then she turned, listened and said with a nod, "Your mother. She's forgot her key again. That woman would forget her head if it wasn't screwed on tight."

Nora caught her breath at the deliberate impudence in Mattie's voice as she moved toward the front door. Three months ago, before the death of Nora's father, Mattie would not have dared speak thus. But now—Nora's hand shook slightly as she poured a cup of tea for herself.

She heard her mother's light, pretty voice as she said something gay to Mattie and came into the big drawing room, followed by a grinning taxi driver so laden with packages and boxes that he could barely see over them.

"Oh," fluted Celia gaily, "there you are, darling! Do pay the nice taxi man—I haven't a cent! And a nice big tip; he's been a lamb about driving me around and waiting for me."

She smiled at the taxi man and indicated a big sofa.

"Just put them down there, Joe," she said.

"Yes, ma'am," said the driver, a wide grin splitting his dark face.

"How much?" Nora asked, and her tone was curt.

"That'll be seven dollars and eighty-five cents, miss, with tax," said the driver. And as Nora opened her bag, Celia, laughing gaily, reached into it, abstracted a ten-dollar bill and fluttered it at the taxi man.

"And do keep the change, won't you?" The taxi man thanked her and let Mattie show him the way out.

Nora watched her mother, slender, pretty, blonde and fluffy.

Celia turned to the mound of packages, saying over her shoulder, "Oh, darling, I had the most fabulous time! Just wait until you see all the pretties I've bought for both of us."

Nora put her hands on her mother's that were busily untying a large box with the golden monogram of the city's most expensive shop across one corner.

"Don't open them, Mother. They'll have to be returned," Nora stated flatly.

Celia straightened, her blue eyes flashing, her mouth thinning.

"My dear girl, are you completely out of your mind?" she demanded. "After I spent the most wearisome day finding thcm—"

"Nevertheless, Mother, they have to be returned, because we can't afford them," Nora insisted firmly.

"Oh, that's nonsense! I charged them, of course," Celia protested.

"And that's why they have to go back," Nora insisted, and her voice sharpened a little. "Mother, can't you get it through your head that we are broke? That we're practically penniless? That we can't afford to run up a lot of bills?"

Celia laughed gaily, though her eyes that were so deeply blue did not warm.

"Oh," she said airily with a little wave of her well-kept hand, "I've taken care of all that, darling. All you have to do is sign some papers, and we can have things as they were before your poor father died."

Nora said sharply, "Then you *are* willing to sell?"

Celia's delicately arched brows went up, and there was a hint of displeasure in the not quite so musical voice.

"Certainly not, you foolish girl!" she scolded. "Why your father wanted to make that absurd will, giving you so much control—"

"Then just how had you planned to get all this money?" Nora cut in.

"Why, by borrowing, of course."

"You mean putting a mortgage on the property?"

"Well, of course." Celia carefully avoided meeting Nora's eyes. "I've already talked to Bob Burke at the bank. Of course we can only make a loan for a small part of what the property is really worth, but it will see us through until—"

"Until?" Nora repeated as her mother's voice faded slightly.

"Until you make a suitable marriage, of course. Why not?" And now Celia was definitely snapping at her. "You can marry Brock Neilson tomorrow if you want to."

"Which I don't. And that's just dandy, because Brock is almost as broke as we are and is definitely not a man to marry a girl in my financial position," Nora answered sharply.

"Oh, well, you're beautiful, and our family is one of the oldest and best in the whole south, so there shouldn't be any difficulty at all about your making a suitable marriage. And to do that you have to have proper clothes and be able to appear in the right places."

"Mother, we are *not* going to put a mortgage on the place, and I have found a job," Nora delivered her ultimatum in a tone that told Celia her mind was firmly made up.

For a moment only the first part of Nora's statement

registered, and then, as she grasped the last words, Celia gasped and her pretty face went grayish beneath her exquisite make-up.

"You *what?*" she asked, as though quite sure that she couldn't possibly have heard such a word.

"You heard me," Nora told her grimly. "I've got a job."

Panic gleamed for a moment in Celia's eyes, and then she laughed, a thin, brittle laugh.

"My dear silly child, what could you possibly do that anyone would pay you for?" she scoffed.

"I'm going to be a bridal consultant at Belloti's," Nora said evenly, and watched her mother's reaction with an almost analytical interest.

"Belloti's?" Celia repeated faintly, and dropped into a chair as though her knees would no longer support her. "With that horrible old Mrs. Anstruther? Nora, I forbid it! Do you hear? I forbid it!"

Nora said quietly, "I'm twenty-three, Mother."

"You're twenty-two and ten months."

"And since the terms of Dad's will forbid me to dispose of the place without your consent, or for you to mortgage it without mine—it seems a very nice solution. The salary and commissions aren't enough to provide what you consider the niceties, but at least it will feed us and pay the taxes on this monstrosity of a house."

"How dare you speak of your home in such a tone?" gasped Celia.

Nora eyed her for a moment, drew a deep breath and decided that she might as well deliver the knockout blow while her mother was in a state of shock.

"Also, I've decided to rent out rooms," she said, and waited.

Once more, Celia was too overcome for a moment to grasp the full effect of Nora's words. But when she did she gave a small, squeaking shriek of such shock and horror that Nora moved a step closer, lest her mother faint.

Rapidly Nora went on, "There are eight unused bedrooms, each with its own bath. Your quarters won't be affected, nor mine. And in a location like this, we should have no difficulty getting good tenants at an excellent rate."

Celia fluttered a perfumed, lace-edged handkerchief before her face as though to wave away an unpleasant smell.

"You can't do it! Nora, I won't permit it—a boarding house—a house with the proud history and traditions of Graystone. You shan't—you mustn't—I won't let you—" she screamed raggedly.

Nora waited until her mother's hysteria had ebbed a little, and then she said stubbornly, "I can't see any other way to keep the place up, can you? Unless you'll let me sell it and take an apartment."

"I won't! Give up my home? Where I came as a bride? Where your grandmother and your great-grandmother came as brides? Nora, you can't—we can get the loan."

"And run the risk of losing the place for a fraction of its value?" Nora shook her head. "At the moment we are clear of debt—even the taxes are paid."

"If you hadn't been such a fool about paying up all the debts your father contracted—" wailed Celia.

"And let the estate be sued? The debts were not Dad's, Mother. Most of them were yours," Nora reminded her relentlessly. "And mine!"

Celia lifted tear-wet eyes, for once in her life not mindful of the havoc tears had made in her makeup.

"Oh, Nora, Nora, you're so hard—so cruel," she wailed.

"I'm practical, Mother. Don't you think it's high time one of us was?" Nora asked gently.

Mattie appeared in the doorway, and Nora had a sinking feeling that Mattie had been an interested eavesdropper on the whole unpleasant, exhausting scene.

"If you're planning to eat dinner here, miss, somebody's got to go to market," she announced cheerfully. "The pantry's bare as your hand."

"I don't want any dinner. I couldn't eat—it would choke me—" Celia wailed dramatically.

Mattie eyed her with derision in her eyes.

"Well, I'm going out for my dinner," she announced. "I just thought, seeing as how neither one of you could boil water without burning it, I'd offer to fix you a bite if you'd go get something for me to fix."

"Thank you, Mattie, but we'll be all right; you go ahead," said Nora tautly.

Mattie looked down at the weeping Celia, grinned and stumped out.

2

NORA GOT Celia to bed, gave her a sleeping tablet, stayed with her until it took effect and finally went back downstairs. The ordeal of breaking her plans to her mother had been an exhausting one. She had known that it would be and she had dreaded it. But now that it was over, for the time being, she felt a certain sense of relief.

She was much too exhausted to remember that she had had nothing to eat save an unappetizing drugstore sandwich at noon.

She was in the small morning room, trying to relax, when suddenly there was the sound of the door chimes. She started up, glanced at the clock and saw that it was a quarter of ten. Uneasily, she realized she and her mother were alone in the house for the first time.

The chimes sounded again as she went along the big hall to the front door, pausing to switch on the porch light before she opened the door.

A pleasantly rugged young man stood there, his red head bare, a somewhat battered trench coat belted snugly about him, the collar turned up. His dark brown eyes were as friendly as a setter dog's as he grinned at her.

"Oh, hello," he greeted her warmly. "I know it's late to be hunting a room, but I was told this was an excellent neighborhood. I saw your ad in the paper, and some of the fellows told me this was walking distance from downtown."

"It's a little over two miles," Nora reminded him.

"That's walking distance, where I come from," he assured her, his grin growing slightly anxious. "But maybe I'd better tell you right away that I'm a Yankee—and if you're a Yankee hater, I'd better not take up your time."

Nora laughed.

"That's absurd," she assured him. "We don't allow Yankee haters in these parts. We're too grateful to the Yankees for bringing us increased prosperity and the like of that."

"Well, now, aren't you nice?" He beamed at her. "And *do* you have a vacancy left?"

"We have a choice of eight," Nora told him. "The ad was placed in the newspaper this afternoon, and there hasn't been any wild rush of applicants so far."

He looked beyond her to the serenely gracious hall, the rooms opening off of it, the gracefully winding stairs and nodded.

"Well, there will be, make no mistake about that," he assured her. "Could I have a room, please, ma'am?"

"Won't you come in?" Nora swung the big, heavy front door back.

"Thanks, I'd like to." The young man looked about him in frank pleasure. "Hi, this is one of those famous antebellum homes I've read so much about, isn't it?"

"Well, not quite antebellum, I'm afraid," Nora told him. "It was built about the 1880s. If you'll come this way?"

She led the way up the stairs and to a white-painted door which she swung open, leading the way into a room.

The man took a swift look about, nodded and said firmly, "I'll take it."

Nora's eyes widened a little.

"Don't you even want to know the rent?" she asked

curiously. "And wouldn't you like to see one of the other rooms?"

The man's eyes took in the mahogany four-poster, with its glazed chintz curtains that matched the floor-length draperies at the windows; the solidly comfortable armchairs, the desk beside the window, the open door leading into a large and well appointed bath.

"Whatever the rent is, I'll take it," he said firmly.

Nora asked diffidently, "Do you think twenty dollars a week is too much? We don't serve meals, or allow kitchen privileges, I'm afraid."

"I think twenty dollars a week is dirt-cheap, and I wouldn't know what to do with kitchen privileges," the man told her, reached for his wallet, and hesitated. "Of course you'll want references and all that."

Nora asked uneasily, "Oh, should I?"

The man stared at her, his brows drawn together, anger in his brown eyes.

"Should you? Well, for Pete's sake, don't you know *anything* about renting rooms, girl? How do you know I'm not an escaped convict?"

"Are you?" asked Nora, her eyes wide.

"Well, of course not, you zany!" The man was still angry. "I just got in town to work in the advertising department of a big department store here. Maybe you've heard of it—Belloti's? Hi, what's so funny?"

For Nora had burst into laughter.

"Heard of it?" She laughed. "I'll be working there, too, from Monday on."

The man's eyes glowed.

"Hi, no kidding? That's swell! In the advertising department, I hope?"

Nora shook her head.

"In the Bridal Shop," she answered. "I'm a bridal consultant, or I will be, beginning Monday."

"Oh, that's one of those joints where if a prospective bride's old man can only afford a thousand-dollar wedding, you talk the gal into one costing five times that? You ought to be ashamed of yourself!" said the man.

Nora smiled. "Well, I'm not. I'm delighted to find a job. I wasn't trained for any profession, but I do know a lot of the best people."

"Which means the best-heeled ones, no doubt," the man cut in.

"Well, I suppose so," Nora admitted reluctantly, and added defensively, "Why not? They are the only people who can afford Belloti's bridal service, so why shouldn't I help them if they ask me to? Every girl wants her wedding to be something special, designed for her alone—and it will be part of my job to see that the girls assigned to me get just that. Is there anything wrong with that?"

"I suppose not," the man agreed though obviously with some reluctance. "Was yours something very special?"

Nora looked up at him, puzzled.

"My what?" she asked.

"Wedding, of course. Isn't that what we were talking about?"

"Oh, but I'm not married," Nora protested, and felt her face warm beneath the man's admiring look.

"Good," said the man. "That's what I wanted to find out. I'm not either—of course."

"Why 'of course'?" Nora probed curiously.

"Oh, just never seemed to get around to it, I suppose," the man answered a trifle hurriedly, and looked once more about the big, comfortably furnished room. "May I move in tomorrow?"

"Yes, of course, the room is ready," Nora said, and turned to the stairs.

At the foot of the stairs, he took his wallet out and offered her a thin sheaf of bills.

"I take it for granted you want the rent in advance, so I'm paying four weeks ahead," he suggested.

"If you'll come in the library I'll write you a receipt," Nora told him briskly, and led the way.

The man looked in startled delight at the bookshelves that encircled the room from floor to ceiling.

"You said no kitchen privileges," he said eagerly. "Does that mean no book-reading privileges, if I promise always to wash my hands very carefully and replace every book I touch?"

"Oh, please make yourself at home here," Nora invited him. "It's my favorite room in the house, too. Some of the books are very old and quite valuable; some are just popular."

"Some are valuable and some are just popular, eh?" He seemed to find that so amusing that Nora flushed.

"Well, what I mean was that some were fairly recent publications my father liked; there are a few current fiction and some biographies, and that sort of thing," she defended herself. And with an added note of briskness, she said, "Now if you'll give me your name, I'll write you a receipt."

"Jay Murphy," said the man, who was moving slowly along the rows of books, speaking to her over his shoulder. "J. A. Murphy, but everybody calls me Jay, because the intials J. A. stand for two names only torture could make me reveal."

"Jeremiah Aloysius?" Nora said teasingly, as she wrote.

"Worse, much worse," he assured her firmly, and came back to the desk to accept the slip of paper she held out to him. He stood for a moment looking down at her, studying her. "My references are all out of town, since I didn't arrive here until today; but we'll consider my tenancy merely temporary until you have time to check the out of town references."

Nora looked up at him, smiling, her hands folded on the desk top.

"Somehow, I don't think I'll need to check the references," she told him quietly. "I'm sure your personnel director at Belloti's must have done that; so if you don't prove to be a desirable tenant, you won't last long."

"I suppose you'll pitch me out on my neck in that event?" Jay mused aloud.

"Something like that," Nora told him, and stood up.

"Would I dare ask you to come out to one of the neighborhood joints for coffee?" he asked so suddenly that she knew he must have been turning the idea over and over in his mind. "Of course you don't know me from Adam's off-ox, but since we are going to be sharing living quarters in this house, couldn't that be accepted as a sort of introduction? I'm just beginning to remember that I've had no dinner, so if you don't want me to starve to death on your doorstep, why not come along with me and tell me which of the nearby places are least certain to poison a fellow?"

Nora laughed. "I'd like to, very much, because I suddenly remember I've had no dinner either."

Jay's eyes were brown and eager.

"Then what are we waiting for?" he demanded eagerly. "Come on!"

"I can't leave my mother alone in the house, and all the servants are out," Nora answered with frank disappointment.

"Oh?" Jay's face fell. "What time are the servants due back?"

"Only one of them is, and that's any time it occurs to her," Nora admitted ruefully. "The others are gone for good, to other jobs."

As she came out into the big reception hall with him, there was the distant slam of a door, then heavy footsteps behind the service door, which swung open to reveal Mattie, still in her big heavy coat with a scarf tied about her head.

Her eyes sped from Nora to Jay and held a lively twinkle of curiosity.

"Just wanted you to know I was back, Miss Nora," she announced, "so's you and the madam wouldn't think you were all alone in the house."

"Thank you, Mattie," said Nora, and added impulsively, "Then if you are going to be here with Mother, I'll go across the street with Mr. Murphy and have a sandwich."

"You do that, Miss Nora. I'll look out for your mother," Mattie said cheerfully.

The door closed behind them and they stepped out into the cold night.

"Sunny South, huh?" Jay complained as he turned his coat collar higher and shivered. "I came south expecting to be beguiled by magnolias in the moonlight and sun-drenched days of lazy warmth and stuff."

Nora laughed at him. "My dear man," she mocked, "this is February."

"So?"

They were waiting for the traffic light at the corner, and he looked down at her expectantly.

"Well, the magnolias don't bloom until late May or June," she answered. "And the sun-drenched days will be here, don't you worry. You'll be sorry you ever yearned for them before summer's over, I warn you."

The light changed and they crossed to the big cafeteria set importantly between two small dress shops, with a huge five-and-ten just beyond it and a supermarket on the corner.

Jay paused at the door of the cafeteria and looked about him.

"A very handsome shopping center; smack dab in the middle of it, that stately old home of yours. How come?" he demanded frankly.

Nora shrugged as she led the way inside.

"Family tradition, I suppose," she said ruefully as they armed themselves with trays and moved along the serving counter. "Nobody was willing to sell, not even when the city kept creeping closer and closer. Mother won't sell even now; and I can't, unless she consents."

Jay nodded his understanding. As they reached the cashier's desk, Nora reached into her coat pocket for her wallet, and Jay stopped her.

"Don't you dare!" His voice was unexpectedly sharp.

Nora flushed and said, "Dutch treat, surely?"

"On my first night in the romantic, storied South? My

first date with a Southern gal? It's not very likely I'd allow that, is it?"

The cashier was eyeing him with a lively interest, a faintly amused smile on her thin, tired face, and Nora turned away, carrying her tray to a table against the wall.

When Jay joined her and took his place opposite her, he studied her for a curious moment.

"My first date with a Southern gal," he repeated thoughtfully.

"You sound as if Southern gals were a breed apart," Nora said swiftly. "What did you expect? That we all went around wearing hoop-skirts and fluttering our eye-lashes and swooning at the slightest provocation?"

"Well, no," Jay answered thoughtfully. "I'm not that big a fool. I have heard some pretty exciting stories about you: that you're radiantly beautiful, possessed of a wicked amount of charm, that you have ways of getting whatever you want from some besotted male."

"Somehow," Nora cut in, and there was a touch of resentment in her eyes, "I'm getting the impression that you don't admire us very much."

"Then why would I have given up a job in Chicago, that paid a heck of a lot more than I was able to pry from Belloti, if it wasn't that I yearned to meet some Southern gals and see if they really *were* as alluring and devastating as rumor hath it?"

"Well, if you've only met me, then you have a lot more research to do before you can make up your mind about that," Nora pointed out.

"Eat your dinner before it gets cold," Jay ordered her cheerfully. "Oh, I'll do a lot more research, of course. But I'm already sold, just having met you. I'm con-vinced all I've heard is quite true—only I probably haven't heard the half of it."

"You make me very curious," Nora admitted. "Tell me some of the things you've heard about us."

"For one thing, I'm crazy about that accent of yours," he told her.

Nora's head went up and there was a spark in her eyes. "I don't have an accent," she flashed.

"Well, we'll talk about something else, then," he suggested lightly. "Let's talk about you."

Nora shook her head, still quite pink from the admiration she could not help seeing in his eyes.

"Let's talk about you," she countered. "Seriously, what brought you South? Since you say you made more money in Chicago—"

"Oh, a fellow gets restless," Jay dismissed the question carelessly. "One day when a howling blizzard was screaming its head off across the Lake, and snow was piled so high not even a stilt-walker could get over it, I came into the office. And by the time I got thawed out, somebody tipped me off to a rumor that there was an opening in the advertising department of Belloti's. I snapped at it. And here I am!"

"And now you wish you were back in Chicago?" Nora asked curiously. "This is a very unusual cold wave we're having down here; it will warm up in a few days."

She broke off with a laugh as Jay grinned at her.

"Are you sure you work for Belloti's? Sounds more like you were on the payroll of the Chamber of Commerce," he teased.

"Well, every citizen of our town *is* an unofficial booster," Nora protested warmly. "We're convinced we have the finest climate, the best citizens, the most beauty. Well, we *do*, and you've no right to laugh! You just wait; if you stay, you'll soon start being a booster, too. That's how we were able to rebuild after we were burned to the ground in the War Between the States. If we hadn't had faith, and hadn't worked like demons, we'd still be a small-town crossroads!"

"So there!" Jay mocked her. "I always feel that if a city has people who believe in it and its future and are willing to fight for it, it's a darned good city to live in!"

"Well, thanks!" Nora turned back to her dinner, somewhat mollified. "You just wait until the dogwoods bloom

—there are more than fifteen thousand of them all over the city! And—oh, stop laughing at me!"

"My dear sweet girl," said Jay, and his tone was only faintly touched with raillery, "I'm not laughing at you; I'm laughing *with* you! And that's the way friendships begin."

3

In the morning, Nora peeped into her mother's room, but Celia was sleeping soundly. She went out and down the stairs and back to the service quarters, from which, as she pushed open the door, she caught the heartening smell of coffee.

Mattie looked up from the kitchen table where she sat above a plate of buttered toast and a steaming cup of coffee.

"Good morning, Mattie," said Nora pleasantly, "that smells like delicious coffee. Would you have enough for me to have a cup?"

Mattie's skin flushed darkly, and there was a shamed look in her eyes as she stood up swiftly and went to get another cup and a plate.

"Would you like it in the dining room, miss?" she asked awkwardly.

"Don't be silly, Mattie. Can't I have it here with you?"

Mattie put down the cup of coffee and slid two slices of bread into the toaster before she took her own place again.

"You know, Miss Nora, I'm downright ashamed of the way we've all behaved since your father died," she said impulsively, "running out on you the minute we found you couldn't keep on paying us the fancy salaries we have been getting. But—well, folks have to look out for their own interests, I suppose."

"Of course you do, Mattie, and I don't blame you a bit," Nora assured her quite sincerely. "Mother and I can't afford a staff of servants any longer, and we were glad you could all find good jobs so quickly."

Mattie nodded. "Oh, with the servant problem the way it is nowadays, nobody needs to be out of work if they're well-trained and willing to work," she agreed, and added curiously, "But what are you and the madam going to do, Miss Nora? You're not going to live here in this big old house all by yourselves?"

"Of course not, Mattie," Nora answered. "I've got a job, and we're going to rent out rooms."

Mattie gasped.

"Miss Nora, you're kiddin'!"

"The young man you saw last night is our first tenant," Nora said firmly. "And I'm going to work at Belloti's on Monday."

"Well, forevermore!" murmured Mattie, awed and astounded.

"There is a problem, of course, Mattie."

"Usually there is," Mattie agreed warily.

"There will be eight bedrooms and baths to be cleaned and kept in order, in addition to the rest of the house," Nora pointed out. "I won't have time to do it properly, and I can't afford to pay top wages."

"I'm real sorry I've already promised the Pearsons I'd start work there Monday," Mattie said hurriedly, her eyes refusing to meet Nora's.

"Heavens, Mattie, I wasn't trying to entice you to stay on," Nora said swiftly. "The Pearsons have taken almost the whole staff, so you'll be with your friends. I just thought possibly you might know of somebody I could get: a woman who would do the cleaning and get lunch for Mother when she is at home. It would have to be somebody who wouldn't expect to be paid anything like what the Pearsons are happy to pay you, because I wouldn't be able to afford it."

Mattie hesitated a moment, studying Nora, and then she said slowly, thoughtfully, "Well, the only one I can think of is my niece, Emma Westberry. She's not a trained house servant, but she's a willing worker and as clean as a pin. She's worked hard all her life; she had to, with a drunken sot of a husband and a raft of kids to bring up. Now they're married and Emma's a widow. She has to live with her married son, and she don't get on good with his wife. There are children, and they are all pretty crowded. Emma stays there because she has no other place to go."

Nora asked eagerly, "Do you think she'd like to come here and work, Mattie?"

"She just might," Mattie said slowly. "Matter of fact, I think she'd jump at the chance. But there's just one thing."

"What, Mattie?"

Mattie met her eyes straightly.

"Your mother won't like her, Miss Nora."

"Why not, Mattie? There's nothing wrong with her, is there?"

"Sakes alive, no! she's a plain, honest countrywoman that never had much schooling. But your mother isn't going to like having an untrained servant around."

"No, I guess she won't," Nora admitted wryly. "How soon can you get in touch with Mrs. Westberry?"

"I could telephone her," suggested Mattie. "It's a long distance call, though. Maybe I should wait until after six."

"Nonsense! You go call her right this minute and see if she will come, and how soon," Nora begged. Mattie nodded and left the room.

Above Nora's head a bell rang sharply, and Nora, startled, turned to see that the summons was from her mother's room, indicating that Celia was ready for her breakfast and expected to have it, as usual, in bed.

Nora examined the percolator from which she and Mattie had had their coffee. It was still hot, and there was a cupful left. She hesitated a moment, and then she poured it into a small silver pot, arranged toast beneath a silver cover, placed it all on a tray, and with her mouth a thin taut line, went up the steps carrying the tray.

Celia was propped up against her pillows, fresh and radiant in a vastly becoming bed jacket, her golden hair brushed back from her face and held in place with a youthful ribbon band.

"Oh," she said as Nora came in with the tray. "Why didn't you send Mattie up with it?"

"Mattie's busy," said Nora briefly, and put the tray in place across her mother's knees.

Celia shook out the crisp linen napkin, poured coffee into the egg-shell china cup, and looked outraged that the cup was not quite full.

"I'm sorry, Mother, but that's all the coffee that was left," Nora explained. "I have to go marketing this morning and get in some supplies."

Celia daintily tasted the coffee, made an outraged grimace and pushed it away.

"Take the horrible stuff away! Toast without butter— and that horrible warmed over coffee."

"Well, as soon as we get a few more rooms rented," Nora reminded her deliberately, "and when I get my first salary check—"

Celia looked up at her like a frightened, woebegone child who cannot believe that Santa Claus overlooked her on Christmas Eve.

"Oh, yes, I do recall your mentioning some nonsense about a job and renting rooms. You couldn't possibly have meant it, Nora."

Nora removed the tray and stood looking down at her mother, her eyes weary but her chin and her mouth set stubbornly.

"I never meant anything more, Mother," she said grimly. "I rented a room last night, to a young man who works at Belloti's."

Celia quailed as though she had had a terrific and undeserved blow.

"Oh, Nora darling, you didn't!" she whimpered.

Nora nodded, hands jammed deeply into the pockets of her thick sweater.

"I did, Mother," she insisted. "And I hope that the ad in the paper will rent the other seven before Monday."

Celia was too shocked, too overwhelmed to comment. She could only recoil against her lacy silk-and-satin pillows, in her expensive bedjacket, and stare at Nora with horrified eyes.

"Mattie is trying to find us a housekeeper now," Nora went on. "She thinks her niece will be glad of a job taking care of the house and looking after you, giving you lunch when you want it, and I suppose preparing dinner for us at night. I'll prepare my own breakfast, of course, before I go to work."

Celia flung up her dainty hands in horror.

"Oh, Nora, Nora, how can you do this to me, *your own mother!* You don't care how this all affects me. You're a stubborn, hard-headed, ungrateful girl! How *can* you?"

"Because, Mother, I can't think of anything else to do —can you?"

Celia flung her an ugly glance.

"Of course I can, if only you weren't so stubborn!"

"Meaning the mortgage, of course?"

"Well, why not, I'd like to know?"

"Only because if we were unable to pay it, we'd lose the property for a fraction of its value," Nora pointed out wearily as she had done so many times since her father's death. "If you'd be practical—"

"Which means if I'd let you sell our home and go live in a horrible little apartment—" Celia's voice was ragged, shaking with helpless anger. "Well, I won't."

Nora shrugged, lifted the tray from the bedside table and turned toward the door, as Mattie knocked and came in with a sheaf of letters in her hand.

"The morning mail, ma'am," she said to Celia without expression. She turned to Nora and took the tray, her eyes registering her sympathy.

Celia riffled hastily through the mail, gave a little gasp of delight as she found a letter she had obviously been looking for. She ripped open the envelope and her eyes scanned the letter while Nora watched her, puzzled and apprehensive.

Celia gave a little girlish gurgle of joy, flung back the covers and slipped out of bed, her pretty, carefully tended feet feeling for the satin slippers with their fluff of fur.

"Oh, Nora, the most wonderful thing," she caroled gaily. "Aunt Alicia has invited me to spend an indefinite time with her at Palm Beach. Isn't that wonderful?"

Nora said, startled, "But, Mother, you know you loathe Aunt Alicia."

Celia gave her a bitter glance.

"Not half as much as I would loathe seeing my beautiful, beloved home turned into a rooming house." Her mouth contorted at the words as though they had an unpleasant taste. "Or even seeing my daughter, for whom I had such high hopes, trotting off to work like a shopgirl."

Nora asked quietly, "Mother, did you ask Aunt Alicia to invite you?"

Celia's head went up and her eyes were cold.

"And what if I did? Isn't it time she did something for us? After all, she always insisted your father was her favorite nephew," she snapped. "She'd invite you, I'm sure, if you weren't so stiff-necked and stubborn. After all, I suppose she's lonely."

"Aunt Alicia lonely? Mother, you're out of your mind! You know she is so busy running things, bossing everything and everybody, that she barely has time to sleep!"

"Well, be that as it may, I'm going, and just as fast as I can pack," Celia insisted. "Isn't it lucky I did all that shopping yesterday? Now I won't have anything to do but pack. Mattie can pack for me."

"Mother, I told you yesterday that the things would have to be returned."

"Oh, no, they don't!" Celia's eyes flashed with anger. "The ones I chose for you, if you're going to be penny-pinching and grubby! But I need the things I bought for myself, because I had a visit to Aunt Alicia in mind when

I selected them. They are all resort things, and I've got to have them!"

"Then keep them, Mother, and I'll pay for them somehow," Nora yielded, and turned to the door as Mattie rapped against its closed panels.

"There's two young ladies, Miss Nora, that want to rent a room," said Mattie. Her eyes, bright with malice, went to Celia, who gave a small gasp, put her hands over her face and turned away.

Nora went out of the room and closed the door. She paused to say to Mattie, "Mother's going away for a visit to an aunt. Would you pack for her, Mattie?"

"Well, now I sure would, Miss Nora, and glad to!" said Mattie, and grinned happily as she went back into Celia's room.

4

THE TWO GIRLS who were waiting for her were at the entrance to the big, handsomely furnished drawing room. They turned, bright-eyed and eager, as Nora came down the stairs. They were girls in their mid-twenties, one a delectable blonde, the other a brunette. They were smartly dressed in suits, and the blonde wore a mink stole against the bitter cold of the morning, while the brunette wore a beautiful cashmere coat with a big soft collar of lynx that framed her pert, pretty face most becomingly.

The brunette spoke first, smiling eagerly. "Hello, Miss Robinson. We couldn't believe our eyes when we read your ad in the paper last night. We'd have bounced right in to apply for a room, except we had dates. I'm Susan Braswell, and this is my friend, Lucy Evans."

"How do you do?" Nora found herself liking the girls'

gay and friendly manner, their air of complete self-assurance. "If you'll come with me, I'll show you the rooms."

"Oh, praises be!" Susan yelped happily. "Then you *do* still have a vacancy!"

"The ad was placed yesterday, and so far only one room has been taken," Nora replied as she led the way up the gracefully curving stairs.

"Well, we work right next door, and if we can find a room here, we can sleep half an hour longer each morning and still get to the office in time for the first coffee break," Susan boasted happily.

Nora showed the rooms, and the girls were excited as they moved from one to the other, torn by the necessity of making a choice. Finally they chose a large corner room, with twin beds, and Susan said firmly, "We'll take it. And here's two weeks' rent in advance."

"I'll write you a receipt," Nora told her as they moved back down the stairs.

When Nora had quoted the rental at twenty dollars a week, the two girls had very carefully managed not to exchange glances. But as, with the receipt in her handsome purse, Susan started to follow Lucy out of the hall, she turned back impulsively.

"Miss Robinson, I know you're new to this business of renting rooms," she said swiftly. "But you should always ask more when two people are to share a room, especially if there are twin beds! You should have asked us thirty dollars. We'd have paid it. But don't you demand it now, because we've already accepted your offer."

Nora blinked and then laughed. "Well, thanks for the tip, Miss Braswell. I'll keep it in mind."

"You do that," Susan said firmly. "Lucy and I have been trying and trying to find a place close to the office, but we didn't want an apartment and we never dared to dream that we could ever live here!"

Lucy, who had paused at the front door where she could not hear them, moved back, once more looking at the handsome drawing room.

"The ad *did* say no kitchen privileges, didn't it?" she suggested.

Susan stared at her. "Don't be a dope—who wants kitchen privileges? What would we do with 'em? You can't cook—neither can I."

"Not me," Lucy admitted. "But I was just wondering —how about parlor privileges? I mean, could we maybe use the drawing room now and then for dating?"

Nora met Susan's eyes and said demurely, "I'm afraid that would make your rent come a little higher. The price I quoted you was only for your room."

Susan eyed her warily, without comment.

"How much extra for parlor privileges?" asked Lucy.

"Ten dollars a week," answered Nora.

"Hi, baby, you learn fast, don't you?" Susan accused her wryly. "Me and my big mouth! So it's *with* parlor privileges, and here's an extra twenty."

Nora hesitated and said awkwardly, "I feel awful about taking this."

"Oh, don't be a goof." Susan laughed. "We were cheating you, practically. We've been living in College Park, and it's the dickens of a ride in every morning and back out every evening. We'll be saving money on bus and taxi fares by living here—but don't you raise the rent again!"

"I wouldn't think of it," Nora assured her warmly. "I'm going to like having you here, and I do hope you will feel perfectly at home."

"You may live to regret that wish," Susan warned her darkly, as the two girls turned toward the door just as it swung open to admit Jay, a battered suitcase in his hand.

"Oh, hello!" His eyes swept the three girls and widened with pleased admiration before he turned to Nora and said, "All right if I move in now?"

"Of course," Nora answered, and was amused at the lively interest in the eyes of the other two girls. "Mr. Murphy selected his room last night. Miss Braswell, Miss Evans, your fellow-tenant, Mr. Murphy."

Jay was pleasantly appreciative and, after a few moments of friendly chatter, went up the stairs. The two girls watched him go and exchanged significant glances before Susan turned to Nora.

"He's cute! Is he yours?" she demanded.

Nora's eyes widened.

"Mine?" she repeated, somewhat dazed by Susan's frankness.

"Is he wearing your ring through his nose?" Susan put it with brutal frankness. "Or is he available?"

Nora laughed. "I met the man for the first time last night when he came to rent a room," she pointed out. "All I know about him is that he's in the advertising business and will be working at Belloti's, come Monday morning. Also, he's from Chicago and unmarried. At least, he says he is."

Susan nodded happily.

"Well, if you have no plans for him—" she began.

"I certainly haven't!"

Susan smiled blissfully at Lucy and brushed the tips of her fingers delicately together, as though she removed dust from them.

"If he prefers blondes, he's yours, pal," she said cheerfully. "But if he likes brunettes—well, we shall see."

She turned to Nora. "All right if we move in this afternoon?"

"Of course."

Susan grinned, glanced toward the stairs and herded her friend out into the wind-driven chill of the morning.

Nora stood where they had left her, staring at the closed door.

Mattie, coming down the stairs, startled her so that she turned swiftly, the money the two girls had paid for their rent still in her hand.

"Looks like you won't have to take that job after all, Miss Nora," Mattie said cheerfully. "The other rooms will rent so fast it'll scare you. People are always hankering to get into these big old homes, with their big rooms and all."

Nora thrust the money into her pocket and said stubbornly, "But I *want* to take the job, Mattie. Did you get your niece on the phone?"

"I sure did, Miss Nora, and she just about jumped out of her boots, she said she'd come so fast! Her and that daughter-in-law have been having a row, I know from the way Emma talked. She'll be here on the six-forty bus, and I'll meet her at the bus station and bring her on out here."

The doorbell chimed, and Mattie went forward to open the door. A man and woman in their middle fifties stood there, and as the door opened their eyes swept over the interior of the hall and the half-open library door.

"Come in, please," Mattie invited them pleasantly.

"Er—oh, yes, of course, thank you," said the man, and added, "Are you the landlady?"

Mattie grinned but answered politely, "No, sir, this is Miss Robinson."

Nora took a step forward and smiled pleasantly at the two.

"You're the—er—the—" The man's voice stumbled, and Nora smiled.

"I'm the landlady," she told him, and thought how her mother would have shrieked in dismay at the word. "You're looking for a room?"

The man glanced swiftly, almost apprehensively, about the stately, handsome old house and said uncertainly, "Well, yes, but first of all I must ask you—that is, I must tell you that my wife is not a businesswoman. She will be at home most of the day, but I assure you, she will stay in her own room and not be a bother."

Nora looked at the small, plump woman whose silvery hair was crowned by a neat green hat that matched her tweed topcoat, and felt a little warm rush of friendliness.

"I'm sure she couldn't be a bother, not even if she tried," she said gently.

The man and the woman exchanged swift glances.

"You don't object to women who don't go to business every day?" asked the man.

"Goodness, no!" Nora was puzzled. "Why should I?"

"Well, most landladies object to having a woman around the house in the daytime," the woman admitted painfully. "And they just won't believe me when I try to tell them that I am out most of the day and I never hang around outside my own room."

"We have our own TV, and Jane reads a great deal, and we go out for meals, and she spends a lot of time in the stores just watching people," the man said. "She won't be a bother, I promise you."

Nora made a little gesture of bewilderment.

"I frankly don't know what all this is about," she said. "I've never done anything like this before. I mean rent out rooms. But the house is much too large for just Mother and me, and with all those extra bedrooms it seemed rather silly not to have them used. But I should surely expect you to make yourselves at home."

The man and his wife exchanged radiant smiles. Nora saw his hand reach out for his wife's, and they beamed at her.

"If you knew how many nice rooms we've found, only to be told that unless my wife was a businesswoman, we couldn't have them," said the man, and sighed at the memory. "I'm Sam Blake, and this is my wife, Jane."

"I'm very happy to meet you, and if you'll come with me, I'll show you the rooms that are still available," Nora offered pleasantly.

Mattie said quietly, "If I might speak to you a moment alone, Miss Nora?"

Mrs. Blake turned a startled face, alarm in her eyes.

"Oh, now you're not going to try to talk her out of letting us live here?" she protested, stricken.

"Sakes alive, ma'am," Mattie protested, "nothing like that. It's Miss Nora's house, and I'm sure she'll be glad to have nice folks like you and Mr. Blake here. I just wanted to tell her if she'd give me the money, I'd do the marketing for her. Looks like she's going to have a busy day here, and I can save her that much trouble."

Mrs. Blake's plump, pretty face was eased of its frightened look, and Nora excused herself and went into the library with Mattie.

"You're sure you don't mind doing the marketing, Mattie?" she asked, as she held out the money she had just accepted from the two girls.

"Little enough to do for you, Miss Nora," answered Mattie, selected a few of the bills and folded them in her hand. "Likely you wouldn't know where to start, anyway, seeing you've never done any marketing."

"You're quite right, Mattie. I'd make a mess of it, I know," Nora said frankly.

"Well, Emma'll do it from now on, so I'll just stock up for the weekend, and you can stay here and rent out the rest of the rooms. From the way folks are coming to answer that ad, there won't be a vacancy left by tonight," Mattie told her briskly, and started for the door, leaving Nora to go back to the Blakes, who were waiting for her in frank apprehension.

"We were afraid you might change your mind," Mrs. Blake confessed humbly, "about letting an unemployed woman live here."

Nora laughed as she led the way up the stairs.

"I'm going to be a businesswoman myself after Monday," she said lightly. "But I have a housekeeper coming in who will take care of the rooms and the house.

"Oh, would you mind if I took care of our own room myself?" asked Mrs. Blake anxiously.

"Would you like that?" asked Nora, puzzled.

"Oh, yes, I would," answered Mrs. Blake eagerly. "I've always kept house. But when the new highway took over our home, and we had to move, Sam and I decided it would be foolish to buy another, since we have no one to leave it to. He had a good business offer here, and we've been looking for a place to live. I do declare, if I'd known landladies were so opposed to having a woman in the house that doesn't go out to business five days a week, I think I'd have tried to learn a profession that would make it possible for me to get a job—just so's they'd have to let me in! They made me feel not quite respectable."

It was, of course, a foregone conclusion that they would select a room, pay a month's rent and depart, walking on air, to collect their belongings and return to settle in.

5

BY MID-AFTERNOON the last available room had been taken, by a middle-aged professor at a nearby college.

Nora bade the professor a pleasant goodbye and dropped into a deep chair in the library. She was tired and worried because of the way her mother had gone off, but she felt a deep satisfaction in the knowledge that she was going to be able to carry out the plans she had made so painfully and with so much thought.

She was still there some time later when Jay came in and paused at the door of the library.

"You look beat," he said flatly.

Nora flushed, put up her hands to her hair, looked down at her slacks and said frankly, "I must look a sight."

"Up and on your feet, girl; we've got places to go and things to do," he told her firmly, as he came into the room and held out his hand to her.

Nora put her hand in his and let him draw her to her feet.

"Such as what, for instance?" she suggested, smiling in spite of herself.

"Oh, such as climbing into your war paint and showing me the night life of your fair city," he told her cheerfully. "And don't be afraid I can't afford it, because I can. Let's say I won the Irish Sweepstakes, shall we?"

Nora laughed, relaxing a little in his warm friendliness.

"I won't be very good company, I'm afraid, because I *am* tired."

"Nonsense! You couldn't be anything but excellent company," Jay countered firmly. "Just sitting across the table from you, looking at you, is as much as any fellow could want. Scoot along now and get dressed, and I'll shake the moth balls out of my Tux and we'll do the town."

"Oh, we're going to dress?" Nora mocked him lightly.

"Well, you bet your life we are—to the teeth, no less," Jay assured her. "You know something? I love that little-girl grin of yours. It wrinkles your cute nose a bit, and I'm sure there's a dimple hiding somewhere near the corner of your mouth."

Nora said with mock sternness, "Sir! You're flirting with me!"

"Well, give me credit for trying, anyway! I've never flirted with a Southern gal before, but do you know, it's very pleasant! It could even be habit-forming—the very nicest kind of habit a fellow could acquire."

Though his manner was light, there was a look in his eyes that was not, and Nora felt her face warming with color as she smiled at him at the top of the stairs and went to her own room.

He was nice, she told herself as she showered and dressed. And it was kind of him to ask her out tonight, when he must have known she would be feeling depressed about her mother's leavetaking.

She eyed herself in the mirror when she had finished dressing and was grateful for the knowledge that she looked charming. Her brown-gold hair was brushed until every strand gleamed; her gray eyes were steady and honest; the honey-gold taffeta frock was vastly becoming. The mink coat over her arm had seen good service. It had been her father's Christmas present a year before his death, and her hands stroked it lovingly as she thought of him. He would have approved of what she was trying to do, she knew. She drew a deep, hard breath and went out of the room and down the stairs.

Jay was waiting for her, and when she came in sight around the turn in the stairs, his eyes widened and he gave a soft, low whistle of delighted admiration.

"Well, hello there," he greeted her. "Where's the fairy godmother with the magic wand? The coach-and-four are waiting, and nobody would ever guess that half an hour ago they were four mice and a pumpkin!"

Mattie appeared at the swinging door into the service quarters and eyed Nora.

"Emma's here, Miss Nora, but you can see her to-morrow." She broke off to add approvingly, "My, don't you look pretty? You take good care of her, young man."

"Yessum," said Jay meekly.

"You two!" mocked Nora. "Jay, please, if you don't mind waiting just a moment, I'd like to welcome the new housekeeper."

"Sure, run along," Jay agreed cheerfully.

Mattie led the way to the kitchen where a plump, neat-looking woman in her late fifties, still wearing a shabby hat and coat, stood anxiously beside the kitchen table.

"Emma, this is Miss Nora," Mattie performed the introduction and stood back, taking herself out of the picture as Emma and Nora chatted for a moment.

Nora's offer was apparently as much or more than Emma had hoped for, and Mattie assured Nora that she would see to "settling Emma in" and walked with the girl to the swinging door.

"I hate leaving you, Miss Nora," she said frankly.

"I wish I could afford you, Mattie," Nora answered.

"Well, I sure do, too, Miss Nora, but Emma'll take good care of things. I'll drop in on her now and then to check up on her."

"I'm sure she'll love that," Nora laughed. "I'll see you in the morning before you leave, Mattie."

"Sure, sure," Mattie answered, and smiled. "Run along now and have a good time. Been a long time since you have."

She turned and plodded back to the kitchen and the anxiously waiting Emma before Nora could manage an answer. After a moment, Nora pushed open the swinging door, and as she emerged, Jay came forward to meet her.

"All set?" he asked, as he draped the mink coat about her shoulders and tucked it warmly beneath her chin.

"All set," Nora answered him, with a smile that made him tuck his hand beneath her elbow and draw her close to him as they went out into the cold, blustery night.

He insisted that they must dine at "the best place in town," and so Nora suggested the Biltmore. As they were escorted to their table by a *maitre d'* who had greeted Nora by name, Jay grinned at her.

"Nice to be seen around with a VIP," he told her.

Nora laughed, and looked about the big room where so much of her happy debutante year had been spent.

"Oh, I haven't been here in more than a year," she disclaimed Jay's assumption. "I think *maitre d's* like Julian are paid as much for being able to remember names and faces as for any other skills they may possess. I suspect Julian of taking memory courses in his spare time."

They were in the midst of ordering when a party of six appeared at the steps leading down into the dining room, and Nora glanced up at the sound of their gaiety and went a little tense.

Jay followed the direction of her eyes, looked back at her curiously and finished giving their order.

Julian led the party in an impressive manner that indicated their importance in his esteem. As they were passing the table where Nora and Jay sat, the girl who was in the lead paused, her eyes widening as she looked into Nora's eyes.

Her dark eyes swept over Nora and on to Jay, and her black, beautifully coiffed head was held high.

"Why, Nora," she purred sweetly, "where have you been? It's been ages since I've seen you."

"Hello, Allene," said Nora quietly. "I've been busy."

Allene's thin-lipped mouth beneath its deft make-up curled, and the malice in her eyes deepened.

"Oh, yes, I heard—you poor dear!" she said sweetly. Her eyes swept over the honey-gold dress and she added, "You're looking well. I always loved that dress on you."

"Thanks, Allene," Nora answered. Her eyes went over Allene, in an elaborately cut gown of blue-green beneath a coat of white mink. "You're looking well, too. Not many girls could wear that shade, but it looks quite nice on you."

There was a note of innocent surprise in Nora's voice that brought a flick of anger to Allene's eyes before she turned and swept her party on in Julian's wake.

The man who was last in the party paused beside Nora and said quietly, "Hello, Nora."

Jay, watching Nora, saw the color rise in her face as she looked up at the man. Tall, devastatingly good-looking, superbly tailored and groomed, his face darkly sun-tanned, the man was looking down at Nora with a touch of anxiety in his eyes.

"Oh, hello, Brock. I didn't know you were back in town," said Nora smoothly. She indicated Jay and said crisply, "Mr. Neilson, Mr. Murphy."

Brock nodded at Jay and turned back to Nora.

"I'd like to see you soon, Nora," he offered anxiously.

Before Nora could answer, Allene called curtly, in a tone that made some of the other diners glance curiously from her to Brock, "We're waiting, Brock!"

Nora saw the faint flush that was visible even beneath Brock's sun-tan as he murmured an apology and went on to join the party.

Jay watched him curiously until the group had been settled, and then he turned back to Nora.

"Charming people," he drawled, "especially the cat. But I think you won that round."

Nora set her teeth hard, and beneath the edge of the table, her hands were gripped tightly.

"I don't know what you mean," she stammered, her voice stifled.

"Sure you do! The gal was out to get you with her sharp, nicely honed claws, but you gave her as good as she sent," Jay retorted. "The tall, dark and devastating gent sure jumped through the hoop when she cracked the whip, didn't he? I hope he isn't a friend of yours."

"He was," Nora admitted painfully.

"And you wish that he were again?" probed Jay deliberately.

"Of course not," Nora flared hotly.

"In other words, I should keep my big mouth shut and mind my own business, eh?" Jay leaned back as the waiter came, serving the first course of their dinner.

He changed the subject. And gradually, as he rattled on, obviously giving her a chance to pull herself together, Nora turned grateful eyes on him and managed a smile. Jay beamed at her.

"That's better," he applauded her. "For a minute there, you had me worried."

"Worried?"

Jay nodded, his eyes holding hers. "I was worried that you were going to dissolve in tears and have to be removed from the joint."

"Oh, for goodness' sake!" Nora gasped, halfway between laughter and outrage. "Why should I, I'd like to know?"

"Well, it's a simple matter of arithmetic," Jay pointed out. "A fellow who used to be a friend of yours, and a gal who is obviously out to stick a knife in your back, nice and deep. When she cracks the whip, your former boy friend leaps like a startled deer and you look as if you'd been robbed of something precious and cherished. Nora, are you in love with him?"

The question came so unexpectedly that Nora caught her breath and stared at him, wordless for the moment. Jay met her eyes, and there was a depth and a sincerity in his gaze that told her he was very much in earnest.

"Don't lie to me, girl," he went on, and now his voice grated slightly. "Mind you, I'm not in love with you yet.

At least I don't think I am. I may be kidding myself, of course, but I believe that if you tell me your affections are otherwise engaged, I'll have brains enough to remove myself from the scene. I hope I'm smart enough to realize that if I tangled with Tall, Dark and Handsome, I couldn't possibly be anything but the loser. So I'd like you to lay it on the line—*are* you in love with him?"

Nora set her teeth hard for a moment, and then she said quietly, evenly, "I mustn't be, Jay."

"That's no answer."

"I'm sorry, but it's the best I can do," she insisted vehemently. "I don't think I am. I know I mustn't be. That's all over and done with."

"Since the ancestral fortunes went down the drain, eh?"

His tone as much as the words startled her, but before she could manage an answer he gave her his little twisted grin.

"Oh, I can put two and two together and sometimes come up with the right answer, believe it or not," he pointed out. "Way I see it—the jerk was dancing attendance on you like crazy. And then when you stopped being a rich gal, he shifted his affections to that brunette—and it could be the best thing that ever happened to you. You know that, don't you?"

Nora managed a small, mirthless smile.

"I'm quite sure it was," she said with a painful honesty that he found very touching. "May we go now?"

His eyebrows went up.

"Go? Let her drive you out before you've even had your dinner? Certainly not! Why should you run from her or from him?" demanded Jay.

Nora looked down at her untouched plate and set her teeth hard.

"You're quite right, of course," she managed huskily.

"We're going to enjoy our dinner, and we're going to dance, and then we'll go on somewhere else, and we'll have our night on the town just as we planned," Jay assured her firmly.

"I warned you I wouldn't be pleasant company."

"And I said 'phooey' with my usual elegance," Jay cut in. "I didn't know we'd run into someone out of your dark and devious past who would upset you. Still, if I'd been the bright little boy Mrs. Murphy thought she raised, I should have, since obviously your old friends would throng your favorite joints."

Nora managed a small, valiant laugh.

"If Julian hears you referring to the Biltmore as a 'joint,' I won't be responsible for his reaction," she warned him.

Jay grinned. "Oh, he's not so tough—I can handle him with one hand tied behind me," he boasted cheerfully, his eyes warm and faintly anxious upon her. "This cat in the white mink, she couldn't possibly be a friend of yours? Or *is* she?"

Nora shook her head. "We made our debuts at the same party, the Hallowe'en Ball. It's where all the season's debs are launched. There were eighteen of us, and we thought we were just about the most important creatures alive. Our parents and their friends all made a terrific fuss over us. We danced until dawn, had scrambled eggs and gallons of coffee, fell into bed and slept until tea time and started out all over again. And of course, we were mixed up in all sorts of charity endeavors and the like of that. It sounds very silly now, but—well, we were young and heedless and it *was* fun!"

"And then?" Jay asked after a moment.

Nora looked up at him, and sadness touched her face.

"And then my father died," she said simply.

"I'm sorry, Nora."

"I am, too," Nora said huskily. "He was pretty wonderful. I wish you could have known him. You'd have liked him. And I'm sure he would have liked you."

"I wish it could have happened like that," Jay said gently, and glanced at the table that was dominated by Allene.

"So you two made your debuts at the same shindig," said Jay thoughtfully, "and have hated each other ever since. Why? Did she resent your swiping her boy friends? Of course she would—and of course you did, because any man in the same room with you two would naturally fall all over himself getting to you. How she must have loved that!"

"It wasn't quite that way," Nora said reluctantly. "It's just that my family has been here since the state was first settled back in 1840 or even before. So we had a great many friends, people who entertained for me, and —well, I was popular and she wasn't. Does that sound very catty?"

Jay grinned, sincerely amused.

"Of course, but very feminine, too, and quite understandable," he assured her. "Yours was an old and well established family. What about hers?"

Nora hesitated a moment, and Jay chuckled dryly.

"Carpetbaggers, eh?" he suggested, and Nora looked up, startled. "It figures," Jay explained before she could question him. "Remember, I told you I read a book once. And there was more than a little about the scalawags who came here after the Civil War—"

"The War Between the States," Nora bristled.

Jay grinned and gave her a tiny mocking bow. "Yessum, that's right—the War Between the States. I must make a note of that. Anyway, so her folks came down in the early days immediately after *that* war, carpetbags loaded with Yankee gold, and started buying up everything in sight at the lowest possible price and built up enormous fortunes."

"Well, it was not a pretty business," Nora said defensively, "taking advantage of people who had made such tremendous sacrifices for what they felt was right—cheating and swindling and—"

She drew a deep, hard breath and tilted her chin.

"Wouldn't you like to dance?" she suggested thinly, her chin quivering, though she blinked very hard to keep a mist of tears from spilling from her eyes.

"By all means, let's," Jay answered, and stood up, smiling as he drew her up from the table and out on the small square of lemon-yellow ice that was the dance floor.

Nora fitted into his arms, he told himself happily, as though she belonged there. And though they had known each other such a little while, he was becoming more and more convinced that that was just exactly where she did belong. But he cautioned himself, as their steps flowed together, that he mustn't rush her. He must give her plenty of time to get to know him.

His thoughts were busy with Brock and his relations with Nora, when a turn in the dancing brought him face to face with Brock and Allene. Brock was gazing at Nora with a look of yearning, and Jay glared at him savagely, so that Brock's eyebrows went up slightly in surprise as Jay danced Nora away. She had not been aware that they were within a hand's breadth of Allene and Brock, and Jay saw to it that for the rest of the dance, more space than that separated them.

It was late—or early in the morning hours—when Jay brought Nora home and stood in the corridor outside her door, saying good night.

"It was a lovely evening, Jay, thank you so much," Nora said with a note of warm gratitude in her voice.

"Thanks for what?" asked Jay.

"For understanding." Nora broke off, made a little gesture that was not quite a shrug, and added, "For showing me such a wonderful evening, of course. Good night, Jay."

6

BELLOTI'S was the largest department store in the South. There were those who insisted it was the largest in the whole country, and this was a claim Belloti's neither denied nor confirmed. It was deemed sufficient that the store occupied two city blocks and was six stories high. The two stores connected by means of a basement ramp beneath the street, a massive glass-enclosed bridge four stories above the street. This bridge was the Bridge of Flowers, and among the city's many garden clubs there was a good deal of rivalry to supply flower arrangements for the space. So, crossing from one store to the other, a customer was so bemused by the color and the fragrance of vast rows of flowers that coming into the Garden Shop from the left or the Bridal Shop from the right necessitated a brief period of adjustment.

The Bridal Shop was a vast circular space, occupying one half of the north side of the fourth floor; a very special sort of shop, with inch-deep pale gray carpet, delicate white woodwork and acres of mirrors and glass. And not a bridal gown or so much as a bridal bouquet in sight.

Mrs. Anstruthers, the Dowager Queen of the city's social life, had an office enclosed by glass panels at the very back of the circle; ranging away from it on either side, like spokes of a wheel, were the only slightly less impressive offices of Mrs. Anstruthers' assistants, her bridal consultants.

Nora, reporting for duty on Monday morning, was ushered into Mrs. Anstruthers' office by a properly efficient secretary, who looked at Mrs. Anstruthers with adoring if slightly apprehensive eyes as she presented Nora.

Mrs. Anstruthers, undeniably stout, unashamedly middle-aged, looked up from the pile of sketches and swatches of delicate, cobwebby satins and laces on her desk. Beneath her Queen Mary hat, her silver-white hair was elaborately dressed. Her faded blue eyes were cold, sweeping Nora with a single comprehensive glance that Nora felt sure must show her the price tag on every stitch of clothes she wore.

"Good morning, Nora," Mrs. Anstruthers said briskly. "Glad to have you aboard. I'm sure you will work into our plans very nicely. Ellen here will show you your

office, and anything you need to know, she will be glad
to tell you. I shan't assign you any clients for a day or
two, until you get onto the ropes here. I expect you to
learn fast, to be prompt and efficient and to ask for help
when you need it. Remember, the Bridal Shop can't afford
to make any mistakes. That will be all."

"Yes, Mrs. Anstruthers, thank you," said Nora, and
followed the secretary out of the office.

"Don't let her scare you," Ellen murmured as she led
the way across to an office that already wore a small black
and gold sign reading, "Nora Robinson, Consultant."
"She's really a lamb, as long as you don't do anything
to upset her."

"I'll try hard not to," Nora said, and drew a deep
breath.

"Oh, you don't have to be afraid of her as long as you
use your head," Ellen insisted. "Now, here are the files."

For the next day or two, Nora "learned the ropes,"
as Mrs. Anstruthers had called it. The cool efficiency of
the whole project was a trifle appalling at first. A prospective bride came into the store, selected her silver
pattern, her china, expressed her preference in linens
and anything that could conceivably be chosen as a wedding gift. All of which was neatly typed away on cards
and placed in files. Thus, when a customer wishing to
send a wedding gift came in, she was shown instantly the
preference of the prospective bride and could make her
selection accordingly. As a gift was selected, it was listed
on the prospective bride's chart, so that someone else
would not choose the same thing.

"You don't have to bother with the filing," Ellen explained to Nora helpfully. "When you want to answer a
customer's question about a gift, you ring a buzzer here,
and one of the file girls will come in and pick up the
memo, check and bring the file back to you. Later, when
she's finished with it, she will take it back. You will be
chiefly concerned with helping the bride select her wedding gown, plan the wedding—"

"I don't go on the honeymoon with the happy couple, do I?" Nora could not keep back the words.

Ellen, said, briskly matter of fact, "Oh, of course not, though you are to help them decide where to go, make reservations for them, see to it that everything is as they want it."

Nora stared at her.

"You mean these people don't even choose their own honeymoon spot?" she demanded.

Puzzled, Ellen asked, "Well, why should they? That's what we are here for. We pride ourselves on our ability to find exactly the perfect spot that they want. There's a file on honeymoon spots, and also on airline and motor routes and ships' sailing schedules."

Nora sat very still, and Ellen, puzzled, watched her.

"Didn't you know what this was all about, Nora, before you applied for the job?" she asked.

"Well, I'm afraid I didn't know we went to such lengths," Nora admitted frankly. "I thought we were just to help them choose their gowns and help select gifts for the bridesmaids, the like of that."

Ellen frowned. "Well, I'm afraid you're in trouble, Nora," she said uneasily. "How in the world did you ever get this job, anyway?"

"Mrs. Anstruthers is my godmother," Nora admitted. It was something she had hoped to keep to herself, lest her associates would think she was being the recipient of favoritism.

"Oh, my sainted aunt!" Ellen murmured.

"Promise you won't tell any of the others, Ellen, please?"

"But why not?"

"Well, they might think Mrs. Anstruthers was being a little partial, showing favoritism—?"

"Nobody who has ever worked for as long as fifteen minutes for Mrs. Anstruthers would believe she'd show favoritism to her own daughter, if she had one," Ellen said sharply. "You're strictly on your own here, Nora—

and I wish you luck, because, baby, I'm afraid you're going to need it!"

"I bet I do, too," Nora said uneasily. "I'll try awfully hard, Ellen, truly!"

Ellen was thinking, her lean, homely face touched with a deep scowl of concentration.

"Does Mrs. Anstruthers know you are completely inexperienced, Nora?"

"Oh, of course. But she thought that so many of the girls who are getting married are former friends of mine, and—well, I suppose she gives me credit for realizing I've got to work very hard and learn very fast, and if I'm not completely satisfactory at the end of my first two weeks, then I'll be out of a job." The words tumbled over themselves in Nora's eagerness to get them said, to remove that worried, faintly hostile look from Ellen's face.

"Well, Mrs. Anstruthers created the Bridal Shop. She's been managing it for years, and she's made it famous, and she does the hiring and firing, so who am I to say you can't make good?" Ellen said at last. "You'd better go through the files this morning. Study them, get the idea firmly in your mind. And this afternoon there's a fashion showing on the third floor—though come to think of it, that won't do you any good, for there will be only one bridal gown shown and it sells for less than a hundred dollars. Mass-produced, of course. Up here, all of ours are custom-made to the client's order and measurements. Golly, Nora, I don't know *how* to get you started."

"Maybe if I just wander around, get acquainted with the other consultants, watch them operate—" Nora suggested.

"It's as good a way as any," Ellen agreed, and sighed. "I'll be in my office if you get stuck. And the files are in that room back of that mirrored door over there."

Nora nodded, and Ellen went back to her office just outside Mrs. Anstruthers' private sanctum. Nora sat very still and looked about her, her heart sinking a little.

There were gay yellow-brocade-covered benches and

settees ranged about the big circular room, and in the exact center a tall white wicker flower stand holding an exquisite bridal bouquet of white orchids. Scattered about the room, perching on the settees and the benches, were half a dozen or more young women and older women, obviously awaiting the attention of the consultants. Each of these, behind the glass walls of her office, was bending attentively to the clients beside their desks.

Only Nora's office was empty, and Nora felt very guilty as the eyes of the waiting women glanced at her accusingly. She got up and fled to the files, hoping she looked as busy and as self-important as the other consultants, so briskly busy in their own glass-enclosed offices.

By dint of deep concentration, study and work, by the end of the week she was ready for a final examination by Mrs. Anstruthers and "graduated" to her first clients.

She sat behind her desk, facing a small, blonde, delectable-looking girl in a powder-blue suit beneath a hip-length jacket of soft silvery mink. This was Penelope Livingston, the season's prettiest and most popular debutante. And sitting opposite her was Mrs. Livingston, Penny's adoring and indulgent grandmother; smartly dressed, every inch the great lady whose social position is so assured that she can afford to ignore it.

Mrs. Anstruthers had introduced them in her office, as "Mrs. Livingston and her granddaughter Penelope, who is to be married in September, Nora. I'm sure, Alma, our Miss Nora can be of great assistance."

Mrs. Livingston, obviously an old friend of Mrs. Anstruthers, had smiled her thanks, and now here they were. Nora hoped that her outward show of cool competence concealed her slight inner trepidation.

"Just what did you have in mind, Miss Livingston, for your wedding gown?" Nora began briskly.

Penny's eyes, blue as forget-me-nots, met hers.

"Red satin," said Penny composedly. "Trimmed with Persian lamb, of course."

Nora blinked, but Mrs. Livingston merely said chidingly, "Behave yourself, Penny. Miss Nora doesn't know you as well as I do. She'll think you are serious."

"Well, how do you know I'm not?" Penny demanded.

"She will be married in white tulle, Miss Nora, wearing her great-grandmother's Carrickmacross lace veil," Mrs. Livingston said firmly.

Penny's pert nose wrinkled disdainfully.

"With billows and billows of ruffles and petticoats, looking like one of those loathsome dolls people used to hide the telephone," she protested.

"Looking as a charming bride should look," Mrs. Livingston said patiently.

Nora stood up and selected some beautifully tinted sketches. She said, as she arranged one on an easel at the back of the office, "I'm sure we can find something here that Miss Livingston will like and that will be suitable."

Penny watched Nora curiously as the sketches were exhibited, while Mrs. Livingston gave close attention to the sketches. Penny said nothing. Obviously, she was leaving the whole thing to her grandmother and Nora; but there was a gleam in the darkly blue eyes that warned Nora. The little imp, she told herself, would wait until she and the grandmother had made a selection—and then she'd upset the whole thing.

"I just might elope," suggested Penny so unexpectedly that Mrs. Livingston turned, almost as though she had forgotten the girl was there.

"Oh, no, you won't," she said firmly. "You and Tommy promised the two families that if we let you be married before Tommy goes overseas, we could have the sort of wedding we've always planned for you. We've kept our bargain; we expect you to keep yours."

Penny's grin was impish and lit sparkles in her blue eyes.

"Oh, we wouldn't think of not going through with the three ring circus you're planning," she drawled. "Think of all the lovely loot—wedding presents and checks and stuff."

"That's outrageous, Penny!" Mrs. Livingston scolded.

"But practical, don't you think, Sweetie-Pie?" Penny asked.

Mrs. Livingston said stiffly, "You've no right to be practical," and caught herself, flushing beneath her deft, expert make-up at the sudden raillery in Penny's laughing eyes.

"Ha!" Penny laughed. "No right to be practical when I'm marrying Tommy? Stars in my eyes and a lilt in my heart and the world all filled with sunshine and the scent of roses? Romance 'n' everything? Well, you just stand a little back, Sweetie-Pie, and we'll show you how *un*-practical we can be! You've been fighting us since we were kids, insisting we 'grow up' before we think about getting married! Well, we're grown up now, and you yelp at me because I'm practical."

"Penny, darling, where you pick up such language I really can't imagine," Mrs. Livingston mourned.

Penny grinned at Nora.

"Trouble is, neither Tommy's family nor mine can believe that we've been in love with each other since we were infants," she confided cheerfully. "Why, the first time we met, Tommy tried to crush my head with a rock! And if that isn't love, then I'd like to know what is."

Nora's eyes widened and she glanced at Mrs. Livingston, who was watching Penny with a look that said this was nothing new and that she had long ago stopped being shocked at anything Penny said or did.

"Oh, of course," Penny hurried to explain, "at the time Tommy was four years old and I was six weeks, and I suppose he had a natural wonder as to what would happen if he dropped the rock on my head. Tommy's always been the curious type."

Mrs. Livingston said crisply, "Penny, stop this nonsense and tell us which of these dresses you like best. They'll be custom-made, of course, and it will take time to get one just right."

When at last a sketch had been approved, and Penny had chosen the colors for her attendants' gowns and agreed about the invitations which were to be ordered immediately, even though the wedding was not until September, Penny and her grandmother stood up.

Mrs. Livingston tucked into her handbag the memo of fitting appointments and smiled at Nora.

"You've been very kind, Miss Nora," she began.

Penny cut in, smiling warmly, "You've been swell! If I'm not the most beautiful bride that ever pranced down a church aisle, dragging my beloved, yelling and screaming, behind me, it won't be your fault."

"I don't think I'll be able to take any credit for your being a beautiful bride, Miss Livingston," Nora began, laughing.

Penny's pert nose wrinkled slightly.

"Oh, for Pete's sake, judging by all the appointments you've planned, we're going to be living in each other's pockets for the next three months, so stop calling me Miss Livingston. I'm Penny to my friends, and either you and I are going to be very close friends before I tramp down the aisle, or we're going to hate each other's—"

"Penelope!" said Mrs. Livingston sharply.

"Insides," Penny finished smoothly, and grinned. "So let's stop with the 'Miss Nora' and the 'Miss Livingston.' I'd like you to meet my loved one, Nora. Only don't flirt with him. Tommy's susceptible to chestnut-haired, gray-eyed females, and I'd just as soon not have to fight you. I'm a dirty fighter, maybe I should warn you."

"Penelope, you get more outrageous every day!" scolded her grandmother. "I can't think how a girl brought up as you have been could possibly be so un-couth!"

"Oh, I can be couth when I want to," Penny said cheerfully. "Only I have a hunch Nora and I are going to be pals and I can let my hair down with her. Do I shock you, Nora?"

"I hate to say this," Nora laughed, "because I'm afraid you've been working very hard toward that end. But—no, you don't shock me a bit. You're just radiantly happy, and I think that's wonderful."

Penny's smile was warm and sweet.

"It is, Nora, it really is. Thanks for understanding," she said softly, and followed Mrs. Livingston out of the office.

7

BUT IF Penny, her first client, was a pleasure to work with, her second was anything else. She was crossing the big circular room one morning a few days later when Allene Larrimore and her mother came in.

"Oh, hello, Nora," Allene greeted her sweetly. "When I heard you had come to work here, I told Mother we simply *had* to have you manage my wedding. After all, we've been friends so long, why, I asked Mother, shouldn't you have the commissions on my wedding? I'm sure they will be most helpful to you."

Nora's face burned.

"You're going to be married? Who's the lucky fellow?" she asked pleasantly.

Allene's airy brows went up with pretended surprise, but beneath them her dark eyes were malicious.

"Why, Brock, of course, darling. Didn't you know?" mocked Allene sweetly, and her eyes on Nora's face were sharp and avid for some sign of hurt from the blow.

"I haven't seen Brock in quite a while. No, I didn't know," Nora managed smoothly. "But I congratulate you both."

"The announcement will be in the Sunday papers," said Allene, and seemed a trifle dashed that the news had not hit Nora the painful blow she had hoped. "But Mother and I thought it as well to begin planning the wedding immediately. Custom-made gowns take a long time, I know, and of course I'm not going to accept the first sketch you show me."

"I'm sure you won't," Nora answered, her tone carefully colorless. "Nor would we expect you to. Mrs. Anstruthers makes all the appointments. If you'll wait a few minutes, I'm sure she'll be happy to assign you to a consultant."

"Oh, but we want *you*, don't we, Mother? We insist on it!" Allene said sweetly. "After all, you and I are old friends, and of course you and Brock were once—well, quite good friends, so I know you'd take a personal interest."

Ellen said quietly at Mrs. Larrimore's elbow, "Mrs. Anstruthers is free now and will see you."

Allene laughed over her shoulder at Nora.

"You'd better come along, hadn't you? We *do* insist on having you as our consultant," she purred.

"Mrs. Anstruthers will decide that," Nora said politely, and went on to her own office.

In less than an hour, her buzzer sounded. When she stood up she saw that Mrs. Larrimore and Allene were still with Mrs. Anstruthers and knew a sinking feeling. But she lifted her chin defiantly and walked, a slender, brown-haired figure in her "little basic black dress," into Mrs. Anstruthers' office.

"Nora, Miss Larrimore insists on having you help her with her wedding plans," said Mrs. Anstruthers briskly. "I've told her I prefer to assign clients to the various consultants, but since she says you are old friends, she thinks she'd prefer your help to that of a girl she doesn't know. Have you the time?"

"Why, I think so," Nora answered smoothly, and met Allene's malicious eyes, the wicked smile that tugged at the corners of Allene's mouth. "If you'll come with me, Allene, Mrs. Larrimore, I have some sketches you might like to see."

Mrs. Larrimore bade Mrs. Anstruthers an effusive goodbye, to which Mrs. Anstruthers gave her usual frosty smile, and then the three were back in Nora's office.

By now the routine of selecting a wedding dress was so familiar to Nora that she simply brought out the sketches and placed them, one at a time, on the easel, giving Allene and her mother ample time to discuss each one before she offered another.

When they had gone through the whole lot and Allene was still finding fault with some tiny detail in each one, Nora slipped them back into the files and said quietly, "I'm sorry, Allene, but those are all I have."

"Then your designer will have to design something special for me," Allene insisted. "Anyway, those are such ordinary things you'll probably turn them out on the mass-production line in a few months."

"Each sketch is an original," Nora pointed out stiffly. "And when the gown is finished, the sketch goes to the bride. It cannot be copied, ever."

"So you say," sneered Allene. "Maybe we'd better go to New York, Mother, or fly to Paris."

"You'll buy your trousseau here at Belloti's, and your wedding will be managed by Mrs. Anstruthers and her consultants, and that's that." Mrs. Larrimore, large, superbly corseted, impressive-looking, quite accustomed to laying down the law and having it followed slavishly, eyed the sketches again. "That Number Four isn't bad at all. I rather like it."

As she displayed the sketch once more, the one chosen by Penny Livingston came into view where it had slipped between two others. As Nora stooped to pick it up, Allene snatched it, held it up and nodded.

"Why were you hiding this?" she snapped. "I like it."

"It's not available because it's already been sold," Nora told her firmly. "It's Penny Livingston's gown."

Allene held the sketch out of Nora's reach and studied it once more, brows drawn together.

"It's much too nice for that horrible little brat," she said sharply. "Give her something else. I'll take this one."

Nora took the sketch from her and tucked it into the file drawer.

"That's quite out of the question, Allene," she said

curtly. "Penny has already had the first underpinning. It will be ready for her soon. I couldn't ask her to give it up now that she has chosen it. I'm sorry if you don't find anything else in the sketches that you like."

Mrs. Larrimore, out of patience now, said sharply, "Stop being a fool, Allene. That Number Four isn't bad at all. Perhaps in ice-blue brocade—or a deep creamy ivory satin—either would be quite nice."

For a moment Allene glared furiously at her mother, and Nora watched them curiously. They were so much alike in so many ways. Allene was tall and only pleasantly rounded now; but wouldn't she, before too many years, be as ample in girth and as violent in domination as Mrs. Larrimore? By now Brock must surely know what he was letting himself in for by marrying Allene. Even with the Larrimore millions that would be his as Allene's husband, was it going to be worth it?

That, she reminded herself sharply, was no affair of hers, and she turned her attention to the job in hand. But when the various details had been settled, with Allene being as tiresome and as unpleasant as she could, and they had gone, Nora put her elbows on her desk and rested her face in her hands for a moment.

She looked up, startled, as Ellen spoke from the doorway.

"Mrs. Anstruthers has a few moments free and would like to see you, Nora," she announced.

Nora faced Mrs. Anstruthers across the vast and elegantly appointed desk.

"Sit down, Nora." Mrs. Anstruthers indicated the "client's chair" beside her desk, and her tone was unwontedly gentle. "How's it going, girl?"

"Oh, fine, Mrs. Anstruthers—that is, I hope it is."

A very faint smile touched the old woman's face.

"There have been no complaints, if that's what you mean," she said. "And I think it is. No, I just wondered how you were settling down among us. I hear very good reports from the file rooms. The girls say you are downright meticulous with your memos."

"I'm very glad," said Nora, smiling with relief. "I do want to make good here, because I like the work and I'm so grateful to you for giving me the job when you knew how completely inexperienced I was."

"Nonsense! I was glad to have you. Bridal consultants aren't easily come by, my dear; not with your qualifications and background," said Mrs. Anstruthers. "I'm sorry you had to have that Larrimore creature to contend with, but they made such a point of it."

Nora smiled wryly. "Oh, I can cope with Allene. I've known her a long time."

"So you know when to duck when her claws come out?" Mrs. Anstruthers smiled. "How's your mother, Nora?"

"Oh, she's fine. She's spending the winter months in Florida with Dad's Aunt Alicia," answered Nora.

"And how's the guest house working out, Nora?" she asked quietly.

Nora looked up, startled, and there was color in her face.

"I suppose you're shocked—" she began, a note of defense in her voice.

"Shocked? Don't be ridiculous, child. I admire you for it," said Mrs. Anstruthers. "Your father would have been very proud of you, Nora, for the way you've taken hold and managed to stay on your feet."

There was a mist of tears in Nora's eyes and a small lump in her throat as she said huskily, "Thank you for saying that."

"Your father was a fine man, Nora. I liked him enormously," said Mrs. Anstruthers quietly, but with such deep sincerity that Nora's eyes stung. "I'm very glad you are with us, Nora. And you must come and have dinner with me some night soon. I'll see what night I am free and let you know."

Nora stood up, murmured her thanks, and went back to her own office, soothed and comforted by the knowledge that Mrs. Anstruthers was satisfied with her work.

As she left the employees' entrance that night, in the surging crowd made up of the store's almost four thousand employees, a hand touched her elbow, and a voice said, "Taxi, lady?"

She looked up, startled, into Jay Murphy's face, and he grinned at her ruefully.

"Remember me? I live in the same house you do, though for all I've seen of you lately, we might have been living at opposite ends of the city," he accused her as he guided her out of the surging crowd and down a narrow side street to the parking lot maintained for the store's employees.

There he guided her to a neat, dark blue coupé two years old, but brave and shining with new paint and neat seat covers.

"You've bought a car!" Nora said foolishly.

"Well, why not? I've already found out that in this town, you just don't rate without some kind of a jalopy!" he told her as he helped her into the car.

"What ever happened to your idea of walking to work every morning?" she mocked him as he slid beneath the wheel and started the car.

"Oh, I found that's frowned upon, too—that is, if you want to rate as a rising, successful young businessman," he told her gravely. "But I'll let you in on a secret. I find I could walk to work in much less time than it takes me to drive it! And the traffic situation—phooey!"

"It *is* pretty bad, I know," Nora agreed with him. "That's why I sold my car. That—and the fact that I needed the money, of course."

Jay nodded understandingly as he edged the car out of the lot, slid it expertly into the south-bound lane of traffic and relaxed slightly.

"Would I be out of order if I asked where we were going?" she suggested lightly, after he had negotiated the movement and they were headed away from home.

"Oh, didn't I tell you? We're dining out tonight," said Jay.

Nora eyed him with a mocking gleam.

"And you didn't bother to ask if I had a date?"

"I was afraid to," Jay admitted. "Afraid you would

have, and I wouldn't get to be with you. I thought when I moved into your house that I'd see a lot of you. But you seem to vanish into thin air when you leave the salt mines."

"I've been stopping off at the library to do research." She chuckled ruefully. "Golly, I didn't know weddings could be so complicated."

"They shouldn't be," Jay insisted. "Only two people are really concerned with a wedding—him and her!"

"Don't ever let Mrs. Anstruthers hear you say that!" she warned him. "We never see 'him.' All we do is tell 'her' what he and his ushers should wear. Our motto is: 'You land the man and leave the rest to us.' We'll tell *her* what he should wear, but we'll have no part in choosing the outfit."

"Well, hooray for the poor hapless critter! Kind of you to allow the poor devil that much choice!"

"Oh, well, we let him choose the girl—"

"Like fun you do! *She* chooses *him!*" Jay protested. "You know, man is the only animal ever created on whom there's no closed season. Gals can hunt him down any season of the year and shoot at will."

"My goodness, but you *are* a cynical soul!" she said. "What gave you such a 'down' on marriage?"

"Oh, I'm not down on marriage. I'm just down on three-ring circus shops like the one you're working in. Aren't you just a little ashamed of yourself?"

It was so unexpected that Nora sat bolt upright and glared at him.

"I certainly am not. That's an outrageous thing to say!" she snapped. "We're very helpful to the prospective bride, who wants her wedding to be the most beautiful—"

"And fashionable wedding expensive, so that all her friends will be green with envy, and will rush forthright, as soon as they can snag a hapless male, to Belloti's, to arrange an even more fashionable and expensive one!"

"And is that a crime?" she flashed.

"Well, no."

"Statistics prove," she insisted warmly, "that beautifully staged weddings give the bride and groom pleasant memories that often make a marriage last much longer than one of the 'hole-in-corner' Justice of the Peace affairs. And we often find that the groom has even more sentimental memories afterwards than the bride."

"Ha!" Jay's tone was fraught with a sardonic mirth. "What you really mean is that the poor guy goes through the affair dazed and in a state of shock, and afterwards, as he begins to regain consciousness—"

Nora eyed him severely.

"I'm afraid I'm beginning not to like you very much," she told him coldly.

"Oh, now, wait a minute," Jay protested, and his tone was warm and pleading. "I was only kidding—"

"*Were* you?"

His jaw set stubbornly.

"Well, not entirely," he confessed. "But don't get me wrong. I *am* sorry if I hurt your feelings, but honestly, I do think the whole business is a trifle absurd, to say the least."

Nora nodded thoughtfully.

"I thought so, too, at first," she heard herself admit, to her own astonishment. "My first day on the job, when everybody was so terrifically serious about the smallest most infinitesimal detail, I found it hard to accept. But now that I've met some of the girls and have gotten into the routine, it seems to me very practical and sensible."

"Practical? Sensible? What ever happened to romance?" he asked.

"Oh, it's still there somewhere," Nora insisted, "between the 'him and her' you mentioned. But in my job, I know only about helping her to make herself the most glamorously alluring bride who ever walked down a church aisle. She wouldn't want that if she didn't want to look her most beautiful for *him,* now would she?"

Jay was cautious. "I've got an answer to that on the tip of my tongue, but I'll leave it there," he admitted. "I don't want to fight with you. That's the last thing I want!"

"I could make out a pretty good case against the advertising business if I wanted to," she reminded him. "About ads that make people want things they have no need for, so they'll rush out and throw their money away like crazy."

"Ouch!" Jay protested. "Let's drop the subject of our jobs, shall we?"

"Since we can't seem to discuss them without fighting, let's!" Nora agreed, and smiled warmly at him.

8

Mrs. Larrimore looked up from the papers on her desk as the butler announced Brock. He came into the room, spectacularly handsome in his formal evening attire, and Mrs. Larrimore studied him critically.

"Good evening, Brock," she greeted him, and her round, carefully madeup face held the smile she always wore for him. "You're looking very handsome. A drink? Allene will be down soon."

"Er—thanks," said Brock, and accepted the drink the butler offered as though he had been summoned genie-like.

"I can't tell you, Brock, how glad I am you will soon be able to take all this off my hands." Mrs. Larrimore's fat, bejeweled fingers indicated the papers strewn over her desk.

"I appreciate the compliment, Mrs. Larrimore, but I'm afraid I'm not much of a businessman," he protested.

Mrs. Larrimore's eyes were cool as they swept him.

"Oh, you'll learn, Brock, you'll learn," she assured him in a tone that he knew meant he'd darned better, and fast. "Of course you'll work directly under the Chairman of the Board and his associates for the first year or two, but by then, I am quite sure you'll be able to take most of the supervisory work off my hands. I'm a little tired of making decisions, Brock, and carrying the whole weight of the Larrimore industries. Even with a board of directors and the Chairman, too much of it is left to me."

Just then Allene made an entrance. She never came into a room. She swept in like a movie star of the old-fashioned glamour days, and always paused just inside the doorway so that the full effect of her splendor could be felt.

Brock stood up swiftly and went to her, his eyes sweeping over her with the practised charm and admiration that was a part of his personality.

"I met a friend of yours today, darling," she cooed sweetly, as she buttoned a long white glove at her wrist. "That little Robinson girl—what was her name?"

"Nora, of course," said Brock, taut-lipped. "How is she?"

Allene's eyes, bright with malice, flickered up and met his and dropped, as she held out her hand for him to button the last button.

"I don't know why I always have so much trouble with the buttons on the right wrist. Do it up for me, darling," she fluted, and added, "Oh, Nora? She was fine. She's going to manage our wedding."

Brock's fingers fumbled on the stubborn button and his eyes were touched with shock.

"Nora's going to manage our wedding?" he repeated as though quite sure there was some mistake.

"But of course, darling. She's a working girl now, didn't you know?" Allene laughed, a touch of scorn in her voice. "And of course she's had no business training whatever, so naturally that old witch, Mrs. Anstruthers, being her godmother, gave her a job as a bridal consultant in the Bridal Shop at Belloti's."

Brock was a little stiff, and she smiled at him tenderly, the malice somewhat marring the warmth of that smile.

"How did she happen to—I mean, how did she know—" Brock broke off awkwardly.

"Oh, when I went into the shop, I asked for her," Allene assured him gaily. "I knew she was there, and I know there must be fabulous commissions for the consultants, and I thought since Mother would be spending so much money there, Nora should have the commissions."

Brock studied her for a moment, and his jaw was set.

"That was like you, darling," he said, and there was no faint shade of warmth or approval in his voice. But Allene chose to ignore the fact.

"Oh, it was nothing, really," she said airily. "After all, Nora and I were once very good friends, and I always say if your friends won't help you when you're down—then what good are friends?"

She smiled up at him, and Brock studied her for a long moment. At something in his eyes, her own flickered lightly.

"And of course Mother will give her a generous tip," she began.

"Which Nora won't accept," Brock said harshly.

"Oh, darling, don't be silly!" Allene laughed that to scorn. "She'll be tickled to death! With that mother of hers—"

Brock said very distinctly, "Shall we go?"

Allene smiled and nodded. "We'd better. We're going to be late as it is."

They had reached the door when Mrs. Larrimore said crisply, "Allene, I want to speak to you, privately."

Brock flung a glance at the woman, nodded to Allene and went on out into the foyer.

"Yes, Mother?" Allene was wide-eyed and innocent.

"Allene, you're a fool!" Mrs. Larrimore's voice was low but savage. "Do you want to lose the man? Break your engagement before it's even formally announced?"

Allene laughed and drew her expensive furs about her slender yet well-rounded body.

"Oh, Brock will never break our engagement. He's too eager to live in the lap of luxury which he knows the Larrimore money can provide," she drawled.

"I wouldn't be too sure of that," snapped her mother. "Stop needling him about Nora, or he's likely to hand you a most unpleasant surprise."

Allene's gaiety fled, and there was a touch of anxiety in her eyes as she studied her mother.

"You think he'd dare?" she asked at last.

"I think he would. He wouldn't want to, of course, but a man like Brock can have unexpected depths of self-respect that are pretty well submerged until somebody hits too hard. So watch yourself."

Allene, who had long ago learned a vast respect for her mother's forthright opinions, nodded reluctantly and promised, as she swept out to join Brock.

Penny Livingston floated down the stairs, apparently completely unaware of the tall, sandy-haired, crew-cut young man who leaned on the stair post, watching her with his heart in his eyes, but with an impish grin on his lean brown face.

Penny became aware of him as she reached the foot of the stairs, and eyed him with lifted brows.

"Oh—er—how do you do," she greeted him politely. "Who are you?"

"The telephone repairman," Tommy answered gravely. "Your phone's out of order."

"Oh, I'm sure you must be mistaken! Why, it rings and rings—"

"I know," Tommy answered. "But I always get a 'busy' signal. Not trying to avoid me, are you, gal?"

Without waiting for her to answer, his arms went out and gathered her close, and Penny clung to him, her young, ardent face lifted to his for the eager downdrive of his kiss.

When the ecstasy of that kiss was no longer bearable, she drew a few inches away from him and looked up at him, her blue eyes ardent wells of shimmering delight.

"You keep that up," she said, her voice husky, "and I just might decide to marry you!"

"Oh, I always wear my running shoes," Tommy assured her, his own voice as husky as hers. And then it quickened and he drew her close again and, with his cheek hard against hers, said very low, "Let's elope! Tonight, in three hours, we can be across the state line where there's a marry-when-you-like marriage mill doing a rushing business."

"Oh, Tommy!" It was a shaken whisper. " 'Get thee behind me, Satan'—and don't push!"

"Precious!" Tommy pleaded.

Penny dropped her hands to his arms and reluctantly pushed him a little away from her, as her flushed face, her shining eyes were lifted to his.

"Tommy, oh, darling—you know how much I want to, but we promised we'd wait."

"But it's all so silly! Why should we wait? We know our own minds, honey. There's never been anybody for me but you, and there never will be."

"And you know it's like that with me, too, darling-sweet," Penny told him, and leaned her forehead against his chin and drew a deep, hard breath. "Darn it, why did we have to be like this? You the only child of an adoring family and me too. They've centered all their plans on us, darling. Gran's heart would be just about smashed if she didn't get to throw an enormous wedding for us— and your folks would be crushed, too. We promised if they'd let us get married before you went abroad, we'd let them give us a splashy wedding."

"And now I can't think why we ever made such an idiotic promise, can you?" Tommy ground the words out as his arms tightened about her.

"Because I'm eighteen and you're twenty-two and they would have done something drastic if we hadn't," she pointed out, and then she looked up at him, her eyes merry. "But you just wait until you see me galloping down the aisle, all done up in a frabjous frock of ivory satin, with Great-Gran's Carrickmacross lace veil floating behind me—I'll be the most beautiful bride that ever walked down an aisle."

Tommy tried manfully to rise to her determined levity.

"Modest little creature, aren't you?" His finger gently touched the slightly tip-tilted nose.

"You don't think I'll make a beautiful bride?" Penny asked anxiously.

"Well, I dunno." Tommy considered the matter thoughtfully. "I guess, on the whole, you won't be so bad. Not if they get you all gussied up in the very finest Belloti's has to offer."

"Oh, you should see what Miss Nora's planned for me," she caroled happily. "All foamy lace and satin—and a blue bustle. I told them you liked me in blue even if it was only a bustle."

"Sounds enchanting," said Tommy, and added curiously, "Who's this Miss Nora gal?"

"Oh, she's my bridal consultant at Belloti's," Penny told him happily. "Nora Robinson. You remember her. Four years ago she was the season's most beautiful and popular debutante."

"Oh, sure, I remember. And then the family went bust —and now she's working at Belloti's. Sounds like quite a gal."

"Oh, she is!" Penny assured him happily. "She's not only going to help me select my trousseau and my wedding gown; she's also going to tell me what you should wear."

"Oh, is she, now?" Tommy's head went up with masculine ire. "Well, I'll wear what I like. I may show up for this three-ring circus in slacks, tennis shoes and a black leather jacket."

"Well, just as long as you leave your motorcycle outside the church, I'll never complain." Penny laughed at the picture, and then the laughter fled and she clung to him once more, her face hidden against his shoulder. "Oh, Tommy, Tommy, I love you so much."

"That's good," said Tommy, his voice soft and husky as his arms tightened about her. "That's the way I love you, too, Chick!"

"You know something?" Penny asked him after a moment that could have been seconds or minutes or more; neither knew nor cared.

"Something," Tommy agreed cautiously. "What, for instance?"

"We're the two luckiest people in the whole wide world," Penny assured him extravagantly, "to have found each other while we were still young enough to appreciate being in love for the first, the last and the only time."

"Well, it darned well better be the last time for you, my girl, because if I catch you falling out of love with me I won't be responsible for what will happen to you."

And all Penny could utter was a small, breathed, "Oh, Tommy, Tommy." Which, obviously, was as much of an answer as Tommy expected, required, or knew how to handle.

9

As THE DAYS slid by and became weeks, Nora found herself more and more engrossed in her job.

Spring slipped in all but unannounced. Nora had the feeling that she had just looked up one day, and there it was: daffodils rioting in the few gardens still left in her neighborhood; a few proud tulips marching along the walks.

She and Jay saw a lot of each other; their friendship was developing pleasantly. There were occasional brief letters from her mother, usually concerned with the gaieties of life at Palm Beach, and with only a small, minor complaint now and then about Aunt Alicia's demands for her services.

She saw a good bit of Allene and Penny, as was inevitable since she had been assigned as their consultant. Penny was a darling, and Nora had become quite fond of her. Allene was—well, what Allene had always been: arrogant, demanding, chary of praise, lavish of complaints. But that was what Nora had expected of her. There were other girls assigned to Nora's charge who were so grateful, so appreciative of Nora's suggestions and help that they more than made up for the very few like Allene. On the whole, Nora reminded herself frequently, she was well content and very lucky to have all the vacancies in the house occupied, and to have a job that was never dull or routine.

Belloti's had five places that served food, ranging all the way from a "Sip 'n Snack" bar in the sub-basement to the beautifully decorated Camellia Room on the fourth floor. A cafeteria for the employees occupied a large section of the sixth floor, and here one day when she had finished a more than usually unpleasant session in the fitting rooms with Allene, Nora came thankfully for a delayed lunch.

She had just settled herself at a small table in a corner, thankful that she had it alone, when a girl paused uncertainly beside the table, a tray in her hands, and looked down anxiously at Nora.

"May I?" she asked hesitantly. And Nora, smothering a sigh because there were other vacant tables and because she had wanted to have her lunch alone, smiled pleasantly.

"Of course," she answered.

The girl placed her dishes on the table, her brown eyes eager, her face flushed so that the large pale freckles were very apparent.

"You work in the Bridal Shop, don't you?" she began earerly when she had settled herself. "I'm Connie Terrell, from the basement. Not the sub-basement, but the main basement."

"Hello, Connie. I'm Nora Robinson."

"I know," Connie said breathlessly. "I've seen you around at quitting time, and I asked about you, and somebody told me who you were, and I knew I just had to talk to you."

Nora waited, puzzled.

"You see, Miss Robinson, I'm going to be married in July," Connie began. "Oh, I could never ask the services of the Bridal Shop, or anything like that. I couldn't afford it. But more than anything in the world, I want a pretty wedding; one I'll be able to look back on with pride and tell my children about. I know I have a terrific amount of nerve to ask you—well, to help me. But I don't even know how to give a small party; and to stage a wedding—well, I just don't know the first thing about it. Could you—would you—advise me a little?"

"I'd love to, Connie," Nora smiled at her. "Tell me about yourself."

Connie's mouth twisted wryly.

"Well, I'm nobody. Neither is Hank, except that he's just about the grandest guy that ever lived," she said earnestly. "We Terrells are a big family. I have seven brothers and sisters, all younger than I am! And my father is a night watchman. He was on the police force until he got badly hurt trying to stop a hold-up. After he got better, he couldn't be on the force any longer, so he got a night watchman job. It doesn't pay very much, but I think he'd just about die if he couldn't be earning something. I'm the only one of the seven old enough to be able to work. The others are in school. The girls are taking business courses, and two of them will graduate this spring, and then they can get jobs, and I can get married."

Her small, plain face topped by red hair was radiant as she spoke the words.

"I know I'm not a bit pretty, Miss Robinson," she went on. "But just once in my life I'd like to—well, to look as nearly pretty as I can. Hank is such a wonderful guy, he deserves a lovely wife. And if he's willing to settle for me—well, I want to do the best I can."

"The Bridal Shop is terribly expensive, Connie," Nora reminded her reluctantly.

"I know," Connie answered eagerly. "But I've been saving pennies and nickels and dimes since I was sixteen. Why, this is the first time I've had lunch up here in over a year. I always bring my lunch with me. But today I wanted to talk to you. Miss Robinson, I have over three hundred dollars saved up for a wedding dress."

"Oh, but Connie, surely—"

"Sure, I know." Connie nodded grimly. "You think I'm an awful fool to put all that into a dress I'll never wear again. But, Miss Robinson, if I could just have something lovely and glamorous, that made me look as pretty as I can, it would be worth it. It's my money—I've saved and pinched—and it's the one thing I've wanted all my life."

"But, Connie, there are very nice gowns in the Budget Shop on the Fashion Fourth—from seventy-nine-fifty up," Nora pointed out.

Connie shook her red head stubbornly.

"I want one custom-made from the Bridal Shop," she insisted stubbornly. "Oh, I know you must think me an awful fool."

"I don't, Connie."

"But you just can't imagine what it means to me," Connie rushed on. "It's something I've dreamed of ever since I came to work here—and that's six years ago. I've made all sorts of scrounging sacrifices, saving pennies. Miss Robinson, please."

Nora put a hand over Connie's where it lay clenched on the edge of the table and said quickly, "If it means that much to you, Connie—of course."

The girl's face lit up with such radiance that Nora felt tears back of her eyelids.

"Oh, Miss Robinson," she whispered, awed and entranced as though some magic wand had swung open a door for her into a Paradise lovely beyond her dearest dreams. "Hank said I would be a fool to try to talk to any of you in the Bridal Shop, but somehow when I saw you I felt you'd understand."

"What does he think of your squandering all your savings on a dress to be worn just once?" Nora asked curiously.

"Oh, he's all for it," Connie said eagerly. "He says we'll always be grubby little people until he gets successful as a lawyer, and that a girl has a right to fling her savings around if she wants to. And I want to, just this once! Afterwards I'll be as sane and sensible and practical and grubby as anybody! Just once I want to be glamorous!"

Nora said hesitantly, "Custom-made gowns in the Bridal Shop, Connie, begin at three hundred and ninety-five dollars."

Connie nodded. "I know," she said quietly. "I waited until I had that much saved up before I even tried to talk to you."

There was a moment of silence between the two. Nora studied the girl, so nondescript, so unpreposessing, yet so deeply in earnest, so touchingly anxious to squander her whole life's savings on this one moment of beauty.

"Hank wants me to have it," Connie repeated. "He's going to pay for the flowers for the church, and we'll go straight to our apartment and not bother with anything like a honeymoon. We won't need a honeymoon, we'll be so glad to have a place of our own. Hank's an orphan and has never had a home. He worked his way through law school at night and drove a laundry route in the daytime, and now he's 'leg man' for a big law firm. But some day he's going to have his own office and a secretary and everything."

"I'm sure he will." Nora found herself deeply touched by the honesty of the girl's frankly expressed emotion.

"And you'll help me, Miss Robinson?" Connie pleaded anxiously. "I know they'd never let me *inside* the Bridal Shop unless somebody like you would—well, sort of sponsor me. Will you, Miss Robinson?"

"I'll do my best, Connie," Nora promised rashly. "I'll talk to Mrs. Anstruthers this afternoon, and I'll meet you here tomorrow at lunch time and tell you what she says."

Connie's glowing eyes, the flush on her cheeks, her radiance was almost blinding.

"The girls I work with told me I was a double-barreled

chump to think any of the consultants would bother with me," she confessed. "But somehow when I saw you, I sort of felt that maybe you would."

"That's very sweet of you, Connie, but of course you know I'll have to have Mrs. Anstruthers' consent. I already have as many clients as she feels I should try to handle."

"Well, I won't have to have any advice about wedding gifts and invitations and honeymoon places. I'll just ask you to help me get my wedding dress. I won't be a nuisance, Miss Robinson—honest I won't!"

"It's going to give me a great deal of pleasure to help you as much as I can, Connie!" Nora promised.

"Now I'll have to run," Connie said. "I'm due back at my station right this minute. Tomorrow, Miss Robinson?"

"Tomorrow, Connie," Nora answered, and watched the girl as she hurried out toward the elevators. . . .

Mrs. Anstruthers listened to Nora, in the late afternoon when the tide of activity had slowed somewhat. And as Nora explained, her heart sank a little as she watched Mrs. Anstruthers' face and her shocked eyes.

"It's ridiculous, Nora—utterly ridiculous!" Mrs. Anstruthers said sharply. "The girl obviously can't afford it, and it would be wicked of us to let her."

"But, Mrs. Anstruthers, if you could have *seen* her, *heard* her— It means so much to her. It's the fulfillment of a lifelong dream: to look lovely just once in her life, for the man she loves," Nora pleaded.

"That's all very well, Nora," Mrs. Anstruthers cut in sharply. "The girl is an idiot to squander that much money, when there are very nice wedding gowns in the Budget Shop, the Fashion Fourth—"

"But she has set her heart on a custom-made from the Bridal Shop," Nora pleaded recklessly, knowing that she was irritating Mrs. Anstruthers, that her job could very well depend on this moment.

Mrs. Anstruthers listened while Nora went on, and at last she said curtly, "You haven't the time, Nora—no one in the shop has. You have your regular clients, and with the approach of June, there are always last-minute pleas from our own clientele, on whom, by the way, the success of the shop depends. Have you forgotten that?"

"No, of course not," Nora pleaded. "I'll work with her on my own time. I'll give up my lunch hour and work after hours with her."

"The sketches are not to leave the shop," Mrs. Anstruthers warned her.

"Oh, of course not, Mrs. Anstruthers, I wouldn't think of it," Nora said earnestly. "I thought she could come to my office on her lunch hour and make her selection. And then I'll arrange for her time in the fitting room."

"I'd like to see Miss Lucy's face when you tell her you expect her to tell her force to handle such a job."

"Well, if Miss Lucy can't fit the time in for Connie, I'll hush up!" Nora promised with an anxious smile. "And I'll do my best to help her select something ready-made."

Mrs. Anstruthers gave a little impatient sigh, and then she smiled.

"You're a very determined young thing, aren't you?" said Mrs. Anstruthers. "I have to admit I like you for it. Very well, if you can get Miss Lucy's consent, I won't quarrel with you. But I still think the girl is being an idiot to throw all that money away, when it would mean so much to her after she's married."

"She says it will be well spent, because it will give her a lovely memory to hold in her heart all the rest of her life," Nora said softly.

Mrs. Anstruthers studied her curiously for a moment, and then she nodded briskly.

"That sounds a bit sentimental, and I suppose the Bridal Shop is the place for sentiment, though we don't see a lot of it here, I'm afraid," she said, and there was a dismissal in her voice.

Nora thanked her and hurried away to the sewing room, where a small, brown, gnome-like woman held sway. Miss Lucy was, the other consultants ruefully agreed, a "terror," as Nora had learned when she had had to visit the sewing room to apologize for Allene, or one of her other clients when they had missed an appointment. But, she told herself now, as she hurried through the room toward the small, cluttered office where Miss Lucy reigned over her domain, this was no time to be afraid.

Miss Lucy peered up at her from a desk strewn with swatches of delicate silks, satins, lace, and behind the thick eyeglasses Miss Lucy's manner was forbidding. "Well, what is it?" she snapped.

Nora braced herself and went into something very like the argument she had offered Mrs. Anstruthers. Miss Lucy listened, her wrinkled brown face expressionless, her eyes, surprisingly beautiful behind the thick glasses, studying her shrewdly. When Nora had finished, Miss Lucy was thoughtfully silent for a moment, and then she picked up a card from her desk, studied it and asked briskly, "When's the wedding to be?"

Nora smothered a small yelp of delight, realizing that Miss Lucy had yielded, and said eagerly, "Any time her dress is ready."

Miss Lucy nodded. "Bring the sketch in as soon as she's selected it and we'll get to work on it," she said briskly.

"Oh, Miss Lucy, you're a darling!"

Miss Lucy looked faintly startled.

"I am?" she marveled, and added, with the first smile Nora had ever seen her wear, "You'll find this hard to believe, my girl, but I was once young and homely and poor and desperately in love."

She caught herself up as though she had said much more than she intended and added, "Run along now, and when she has selected her design, bring her in for her first pinning."

"I will. Oh, thank you, Miss Lucy!" said Nora radiantly.

10

By now it had become a custom that Jay should meet Nora each evening when the vast store closed, and drive her home, or out on some simple date. Tonight when she came out of the employees' entrance, he was waiting for her. As he cupped her elbow in his palm and grinned down at her, someone spoke eagerly beside her, and she turned to find an anxious-eyed Connie there.

"I know you said you'd tell me tomorrow, Miss Robinson, but I just wondered—" Connie began. She flushed as she met Jay's eyes, and took a backward step against a tall, dark, lanky young man who was waiting for her.

"It's all right, Connie." Nora smiled at the girl. "I talked to Mrs. Anstruthers and then to Miss Lucy. But it has to be done during our lunch hours or after the store closes, because it's only for the dress, and there are so many clients who are taking the whole deal that it keeps me and the other consultants stepping. If you'll come to my office at your lunch hour tomorrow and select your sketch and your material, we can get right at it."

"Oh!" The depth of gratitude, the warm rush of radiant delight in Connie's voice were very touching as she turned to the lanky young man, whose eyes behind the horn-rimmed spectacles he wore were very tender on her. "Hank—oh, Hank—I'm going to have my lovely dress! Isn't it wonderful?"

"Swell, honey, since it's what you want," Hank said gently.

Connie turned back to Nora and said, "Miss Robinson, this is Hank—I mean Henry Huston, my fiancé."

"Hello, Hank." Nora smiled at him and indicated Jay.

"And this is my friend, Jay Murphy, from Advertising. Jay, my friends Connie Terrell and Hank Huston."

The two men shook hands, and Connie said eagerly, "I've seen you in the store, Mr. Murphy."

"The name is Jay, Connie," he said firmly. "And where are you holed up in this vast rabbit warren?"

"Oh, I'm in the Bargain Basement," said Connie lightly. "Not the sub-basement—the real one."

Hank said politely, "We mustn't keep you two. Miss Robinson, I'm very grateful for what you're doing for my girl."

Nora asked impulsively, "You're sure you approve?"

Hank's sandy eyebrows went up slightly, and he looked down at Connie as though he hadn't the faintest doubt that whatever Connie wanted to do merited his firm approval.

"Approve?" he repeated. "If it's what she wants, Miss Robinson, then I approve. I want what she wants, always."

"Hey, fellow! Them's dangerous sentiments! Want to put yourself under her thumb for the rest of your lives?" Jay protested, and grinned, "Can we offer you two a lift home? My chariot awaits in the parking lot, champing at the bit to go places."

"Well, thanks, Mr. Murphy, that's very kind of you," Hank said earnestly. "But I have a hunch Connie will want to stay in town for dinner so she can celebrate. This is something she's wanted for so long I wonder she can keep both feet on the ground."

Jay looked from one to the other, his brows drawn together in a puzzled scowl. "I'd be obliged if somebody would let me in on just what this is all about. I'm a stranger in these parts, and I can't follow all this three-cheers-and-a-wild-halloo chatter."

Connie laughed radiantly.

"Oh, Miss Robinson's going to help me get a wedding dress from the Bridal Shop—custom-made!"

Nora met Jay's startled, indignant look and said defensively, "Well, it's something she's always wanted, and now she's going to have it. And if Hank approves, I see no reason why you shouldn't."

"Who said I didn't?" Jay asked, and turned back to Hank. "Since we are all staying in town for dinner, why don't we make it a double date?"

Connie's smile was eager, but a dark flush showed on Hank's jaw.

"Thanks, Mr. Murphy, but I'm afraid I couldn't manage that," he said with brutal frankness. "Connie and I know a cheap little cafeteria where we go when we're 'out on the town.' I'm quite sure you and Miss Robinson wouldn't care for it."

Jay gave a derisive hoot.

"Look, fellow, two days before pay day I feed her at a hamburger stand and take her to a drive-in!" he said firmly. "You'll be my guests."

"We'll go Dutch, or not at all," Hank insisted as firmly.

"Dutch it is. Do we make the girls pay for their own hamburgers?"

Hank grinned. "Well, no, if they don't want a second one, I guess I can manage to pay for Connie's and her fare at the drive-in."

"Swell—then what are we waiting for?" demanded Jay. He offered his arm ceremoniously to Nora, and led the way down the crowded street toward the parking lot.

"That was kind of you, Jay," Nora murmured as they walked.

"Oh, I'm a very kind guy, once you get to know me well," Jay assured her blandly, and grinned warmly at her. "Seems you're a kind gal, too, taking on the little Connie in addition to your other and far better heeled clients."

"You don't think I should be ashamed of myself for letting her spend her life's savings on a dress to be worn just once?" Nora asked uneasily.

"Do you? Feel guilty, I mean?"

"I do, Jay—a little. But, oh, she wants it so terribly."

"Then you should drop those guilty feelings," Jay said firmly. Nora stared up at him, surprised.

"You think I should be ashamed of snaring girls like Allene Larrimore and Penny Livingston into spending a fortune on a trousseau and wedding, and yet it's all right to let Connie—"

"I don't think you *let* Connie; I think her mind was so firmly made up, and her heart so set on this fabulous frock, that there was nothing else you could do. What puzzles me is how you managed to talk the Anstruthers into letting you."

"Well, I admit that wasn't easy—by several million light years," Nora admitted as they reached the car and all four climbed in.

It was a pleasant, light-hearted evening. When it was over, and Jay had driven Hank and Connie to the shabby, run-down house at the very edge of an unpleasant slum and said goodnight, they were all on friendly first-name terms.

Driving back across town to the big gray old house tucked in between the two new buildings, Nora relaxed a little, and Jay glanced down at her as they paused for a traffic light.

"Tired?" he asked, and his tone was unwontedly tender.

"Umm—no more than usual," she answered lightly.

"That's quite a job you've got," Jay told her as the car leaped ahead with the changing light. "I hear rumors of it all the way up to my ivory tower. Of course, I'm not trusted with any of the advertising from your department."

"We rarely have any," Nora said a trifle smugly. "We're so well established in the life of the city that we think advertising a trifle—well, not vulgar, of course, but completely unnecessary."

"Oh, *do* you now?"

Nora laughed and patted his arm consolingly.

"I think advertising is the lifeblood of any business, and your dratted Bridal Shop could stand some!"

"That I deny, pal," Nora laughed. "If we had any more business we wouldn't be able to handle it. We're all working our heads off as it is. I have to find honeymoon spots for three of my clients—some place they've never been—and believe me, that's not easy!"

"If they don't know where they want to go on their honeymoons, then I say the heck with 'em—let 'em stay home!" Jay insisted firmly.

"But it's part of our service—to find the exact spot, to make all the arrangements, buy their tickets, practically put 'em aboard their train or plane! We *don't* have to accompany them to be sure everything is up to specifications, though."

"I'm surprised to hear it!" Jay's tone was sardonic.

"I was, too, when I found it out," she confessed, and for no reason at all they both laughed.

A few days later, Nora was summoned to the fitting room where Allene was trying on her carefully chosen and very expensive gown. Allene was screaming with fury at Miss Lucy, who, secure in her position with the shop, was screaming right back at her.

According to Miss Lucy, Allene had gained five pounds since her last fitting, so the gown was no longer perfect. Allene's contention was that the gown had been wrongly fitted to begin with.

Nora smoothed the troubled waters as she had been so carefully trained to do. Allene was finally convinced, by being put on the scales, and having her measurements checked with those of her first fitting, that the fault lay with her: too many fancy parties, too many lavish meals, too many cocktails. Miss Lucy sternly refused to touch the gown again until Allene had "slimmed off" the extra pounds.

Allene departed still glowering, dropped the information that since she had been unable to find some of the things she wanted for her trousseau, she would fly to New York and shop while she shed the weight.

Miss Lucy watched her go, shrugged and turned back

to her work, obviously completely undisturbed by the violent scene.

"That one!" she sneered. "I wonder we ever took her on as a client, anyway. Oh, sure, she's got all the money in the world and likes to spend it, but money can't buy breeding. And breeding she hasn't got! If she thinks she's going to walk down the aisle in a Belloti gown bulging at the midriff, she's very much mistaken. I'll cut the dress to bits with manicure scissors before I'll let her do that."

Nora grinned respectfully. "I'll bet you would, too, Miss Lucy."

Miss Lucy glared at her. "You're darn' tootin' I would," she snapped, and scurried back to her office.

Nora, too, returned to her desk, where some time before closing time, her phone rang. She said briskly, "The Bridal Shop. Miss Robinson speaking. May I help you?"

A masculine voice said quietly, "You can, Miss Robinson, thank you very much. I'd like to buy a nice seersucker suit, to be worn with a black leather jacket, to ride a motorcycle—"

"Jay, you idiot," Nora said softly, laughter threading her voice.

"Oh, then you recognized my voice? That's nice to know. Look, I have to work late tonight. Think you can get home all right alone?"

"I've been doing it for years, until you came along—so why not tonight?" Nora laughed.

"Always the self-sufficient, non-clinging vine, eh? I'd like it better if you showed just a little disappointment," Jay complained.

"I am disappointed, of course, Jay. But for goodness' sake, you mustn't feel responsible for me."

"Why not? I'd like an awful lot to be responsible for you."

"Jay! I'm busy! Now run along and plan your layout or whatever it is that's holding you up. I'll see you at home later if it's not too late," Nora told him briskly, and put down the receiver, smiling a little as she made herself dismiss Jay from her mind.

11

Nora left the employees' entrance a little later than usual, and the crowd had thinned out. As she swung north along Forsyth Street, a voice hailed her from the curb and, startled, she looked up to see Brock Neilson standing beside an expensive and very good-looking new sports car.

Nora stopped, and Brock came over and looked down at her, his dark eyes troubled.

"Hello, Nora, I've been waiting for you."

Nora's head went up slightly, and her eyes chilled.

"Have you? I can't think why, Brock." Her voice was cool, remote.

"Because I have to talk to you, Nora."

"That's pretty silly, Brock. What can you and I possibly have to say to each other, except that I must congratulate you on your engagement?"

"Don't, Nora," he pleaded so unexpectedly that she could only stare at him in surprise. "That's what I want to talk to you about. Can't we have dinner together? There is so much I want to say, Nora. Perhaps at Luigi's?"

"Are you sure Allene won't mind?"

Brock's wry grin was completely mirthless.

"Oh, yes, she'd mind like the devil, but she won't know anything about it. I've just put her on a plane to New York, and she'll be gone a week or two. So we could have dinner and talk—"

Before Nora could answer him, Jay came swiftly to her from the direction of the store, caught her elbow in

81

his palm and said tenderly, "Sorry I was late, baby. I was afraid I'd missed you. Ready?"

Brock stiffened and anger showed in his eyes.

Nora looked up at Jay, startled.

"I thought you were working late," she stammered, and for some crazy reason she sounded guilty.

Jay looked down at her steadily, and there was an expression in his eyes that she could not quite analyze.

"Oh, I took a dinner break so I could drive you home," he said as though it were the most ordinary remark in the world. He glanced at Brock with frankly hostile eyes. "Sorry, Neilson, we'll have to go now."

"But see here," Brock protested, "Nora was having dinner with me."

"Oh, no, Nora was having dinner with me, Neilson. From now on," Jay stated flatly in a tone that dared Brock to argue the point. And without waiting, he turned Nora about and marched her off.

Short of staging a scene there in the street, Nora was helpless to combat his grip on her arm, or the force with which he was practically dragging her toward the parking lot where his car was waiting.

"I'm ashamed of you," he raged at her, before she could catch her breath. "Where's your pride? Sneaking out—"

Nora wrenched her arm free of him and looked with blazing eyes straight into his set, angry face.

"Why, you—you—" She choked, steadied herself and gasped, "Sneaking out?"

"To meet a man engaged to another gal, who hates your insides, and who would happily stick a knife into you just for passing the time of day with him."

"For your information," Nora raged, "Brock and I are old friends. There's surely no reason why I shouldn't speak to him, even go to dinner with him if I want to."

Jay eyed her speculatively, almost as though they were meeting for the first time.

"Well, no, I suppose not," he agreed contemptuously.

"But I thought you had more pride, more self-respect than to sneak around."

"How dare you use that word?"

"Do you know of a better one?"

"I was *not* sneaking."

"How could you be sure you wouldn't bump into his fiancée at the sort of place he'd probably take you? And from what I saw of her before, I don't think she'd hesitate to stage one rip-roarin' scene if she caught you."

Nora was trembling with fury and outrage.

"There is no danger of our running into Allene, since she is in New York, or rather, on her way there," she managed at last. "And anyway, what business is it of yours what I do?"

Jay studied Nora with cold, measuring eyes.

"Up until about now I thought anything that concerned you concerned me, too, because I had the idiotic notion that I was in love with you. That's pretty silly, isn't it?"

"It certainly is!" Nora snapped hotly. "I can't think of anything sillier."

Jay stood quite still for a moment, and then he lifted his hands, palm upward, in a gesture that marked his defeat.

"That being the case, then it's also pretty ridiculous for me to try to stop you making a fool of yourself over your pretty gigolo, isn't it? I'm sure if you'll hurry back to your rendezvous you'll find him still waiting. He looks like the type that would hang around for hours, provided he felt it was perfectly safe for him to do so. And with his gal out of town, and no danger of his losing his grip on her family's fortune, I'd think he'd feel pretty safe, wouldn't you?"

Nora was fighting against the angry tears that threatened her.

"You don't even know him," she managed.

"Nor do I want to. His kind is a dime a dozen, though. Too bad gals like this Allene Larrimore don't know that, isn't it? They set their value much higher." Jay broke off, jammed his hands into his pockets, and said savagely,

"So go back and have fun. I'm going back to the office. I was willing to risk my job to get you home safely, but I see I needn't have bothered. I didn't know you had a date with him."

"I didn't have a date with him. We met by accident."

Her voice died beneath the sardonic look in Jay's eyes.

"Oh, boy!" His voice matched the look in his eyes as he turned and strode back toward the employees' entrance to the store, leaving Nora to stand there in the shadows, staring after him with wide, shocked eyes.

By the time she had reached home on the bus, Nora had decided that, while she still bitterly resented Jay's high-handedness, she would forgive him if he made a suitably abject apology.

But the next few days proved conclusively he had no intention of doing that. They met inevitably in the corridors of the big old house, but Jay simply nodded, cold-eyed, and went on his way. He was no longer on hand to drive her to the store in the mornings or to drive her home at night. Once or twice, coming in after work, she had met him and Lucy Evans on their way out to dinner, Lucy looking very lovely and preening herself happily. One evening when Nora came in, tired and dispirited after an unusually trying day, she came face to face with a foursome: Lucy and Jay, Susan and a tall, pleasantly homely crew-cut young man whom she vaguely remembered having seen at the store. Obviously, Jay had set up a double date for himself and a friend with Susan and Lucy.

They all greeted her with bright friendliness and swept out of the house, laughing, in fine fettle for an exciting evening. As Jay passed Nora, his eyes flicked hers with a bright, impersonal regard.

When the door had closed behind them and she had heard the sound of his car driving away, Nora stood for a long moment, feeling lost and forlorn beyond all reasoning.

Emma came along the hall from the service quarters, plump and pleasantly anxious to be of service.

"I thought I heard you come in, Miss Nora," she said eagerly. "Would you like me to get some dinner for you? There's plenty in the pantry—and I've cooked some ham hocks and turnip greens, though I don't suppose you relish such plain country vittles."

Nora smiled with an effort. "On the contrary, Emma, I adore ham hocks and turnip greens, but I'm going out to dinner. Thanks just the same."

"Well, now, I thought most likely you would be, same as usual." Emma smiled at her.

Nora turned to the stairs and then back, to ask, "Isn't this your night off, Emma? Weren't you supposed to be off all afternoon and evening?"

Emma looked slightly abashed.

"Well, yes, Miss Nora," she answered. "But if you don't mind, I'd a lot rather stay home and watch TV. We didn't have TV down home, and I do declare, it's more fun than traipsing the streets. I don't have any friends in town except Mattie, and her day off is Thursday, and she always has a heap of things to do. So I'd just like to stay here. Everything here is so beautiful and—well, I'm not much of a one to go traipsing."

She watched Nora anxiously, as though expecting to be thrust forth willy-nilly into the huge city that probably terrified her country-bred heart, and Nora patted her shoulder comfortingly.

"Well, you just do whatever you like, Emma," she said gently. "It *is* your day—and evening, too."

She went on up the stairs to her own room. While she showered and changed from her smartly cut black dress, she puzzled about where she should go for dinner. She was sure of only one thing: she wasn't going to stay in and have a solitary dinner and watch TV!

It wasn't until she was dressed in a very becoming costume suit of jade-green print, the full length duster coat of solid gray lined with a print to match the dress, that she finally made up her mind. She could not go unescorted to the Biltmore or any of the other familiar places that she had once known. And then the thought of Luigi's crossed her mind, and her mouth thinned slightly. It was to Luigi's that she and Brock had gone quite often in the old days.

Luigi himself greeted her with every evidence of delight, telling her how much she had been missed, how welcome she was, and ushering her to a small booth from which she could watch the whole room. There was a pocket-handkerchief-sized dance floor, and a three-piece orchestra furnished music for dancing.

Luigi himself took her order and hurried away with it. And Nora sat alone watching the people about her and trying hard to argue herself out of her mood of depression.

"Hello," said a voice above her head. Startled, Nora looked up to find Brock smiling down at her and indicating the seat beside her. "May I?"

"How in the world did you know I was here?" she gasped, as she moved over to make room for him, and hoped he could not hear the crazy, wild beating of her heart.

"Oh, Luigi is a pal of mine." Brock grinned at her.

"You mean he called you and told you I was here?"

Brock's jaw set a little.

"You may as well know now as later, Nora, that at least one person has been alerted in every spot where you and I used to hang out."

"I don't think I care to be spied on."

"I told you the other night, Nora, that I had to see you, to talk to you, before it's too late," he insisted.

"You know where I live," she reminded him curtly. "At least you used to."

Brock's dark eyes met hers.

"I also know that that dragon guard of yours lives there, too, and while I wanted very much to see you, I didn't have any special desire to have to engage in a brawl with him to do it," he pointed out.

Color poured into Nora's face and her eyes were hot and angry.

"If you mean Jay Murphy—"

"Is that his name? I don't recall that you introduced us that night when he dragged you away from me—and I don't seem to recall that you put up much of a struggle, now that I come to think of it."

"I didn't want a brawl, either, not there in the street less than a block from Belloti's," she said tautly.

Brock was studying her with a curious intentness.

"That's the only reason you let him drag you away?" he demanded.

"What other reason could there be?" she answered his question with another. "Except, of course, Allene. You are engaged to her, remember?"

Brock's face twisted with a savage grimace that was in no way a smile.

"Do you think I'm ever allowed to forget it?" His tone made it very nearly a sneer.

Nora waited tensely, uneasily.

Brock leaned toward her across the small space that separated them, his eyes holding hers, and his tone was low, and touched with a vibrant tenderness that was an echo of the old days when they had been so certain that nothing could separate them.

"That's a terrible mistake, Nora," he said very low. "I know it now. Being engaged to her, I mean. Say the word and I'll break it off."

Nora caught her breath, shocked, appalled.

"Brock, you can't—you mustn't—why, it's less than a month until the wedding date," she protested.

"As if I didn't know!" he growled. "But, Nora, I'm rapidly reaching the point where I can't take much more —Mrs. Larrimore bullying me, insisting I go into the family business; Allene being very much like her mother; both of them trying to dominate me."

"Well, you should have expected it, Brock. You've known them both a long time," Nora pointed out.

He nodded and broke a stalk of celery into little bits, dropping them into his untouched plate.

"But you see, I always thought I was safe from them because there would be you."

Nora was watching him, with the most curious sensation that something warm and sweet was dying by agonizing degrees in her heart. Once she had been sure that she loved this man; that more than anything in the world she wanted to marry him. But now she was seeing a Brock Neilson who was a complete and not at all attractive stranger.

Brock seemed to cringe slightly as though from a physical blow.

"I know what a heel I must seem to you, Nora," he said with an awkward, painful honesty. "I am! But if you'd say the word, I'd break free."

"What word, Brock?" she asked through her teeth.

"That, if I free myself from Allene, you'll marry me!"

It was so fantastic, so utterly crazy, that for a moment she could only stare at him, wide-eyed.

"I know now, Nora, that you're the only girl I've ever really loved," Brock was plowing on earnestly, apparently misreading entirely the shocked disgust in her eyes. "I'm a pretty expensive fellow, with tastes I've never been able to gratify. I thought that with Allene, I'd have all that I've wanted and never had. But I know now that nothing will ever be any good without you."

Nora had managed to get a grip on herself, to subdue the disgust that was welling up in her.

"And what would we live on, Brock? I'm still a poverty-stricken working gal, remember. And my ancestral mansion is now a rooming house which barely supports itself and pays the taxes."

Obviously the contempt in her voice was so well-controlled that Brock was either unaware of it, or chose to ignore it.

"Oh," his handsome face was touched by a troubled scowl, "I suppose it would be a bit rough, but I could get a job."

"Doing what?" suggested Nora with polite interest.

He eyed her swiftly, alarmed.

"You mean, Nora, you mean you don't love me any more?" he asked in childish bewilderment.

"I don't think I ever really knew you, Brock," Nora stated flatly. "Not the man you really are. I thought you were something pretty special. But now—" She reached for her bag and gloves and stood up.

"And now I'm going home," she finished, and waited for him to rise, so she could slip out of the booth.

"But, Nora darling, you don't understand," he protested.

Behind him a feminine voice cooed sweetly, "Why, Brock, how nice to see you."

Nora had time to note the sharp, stricken look on Brock's face as he turned to greet the girl, one of a party of four who had paused on their way to a table and now stood blocking Nora's and Brock's exit.

"Oh, hello, Nancy." Brock managed a hasty smile that lacked some of his accustomed easy charm.

"And Miss Robinson!" Nancy, a pretty silver blonde, smiled at Nora with a look that made Nora think of a cat licking its chops after a particularly juicy meal. "How nice to see you away from Belloti's, Miss Robinson. I do hope you and Brock are cooking up some sort of a nice surprise for the happy bride?"

Nora met the malicious, smiling eyes.

"Why else would we be here, Miss Sutherland?" she asked coolly.

Nancy Sutherland laughed silkily, and her pale blue eyes widened innocently.

"Well, I admit that puzzled me a bit until I remembered you're stage-managing Allene's wedding. Naturally he wouldn't want to come into the Bridal Shop."

She glanced from Brock to Nora, and her smile deepened.

"But don't worry, I won't tell Allene. I saw you all snuggled down together in Luigi's," she promised sweetly. "I'm too grateful to you, Miss Robinson, for talking Allene out of that horrible gown she was choosing for me to wear at the wedding. Being a bridesmaid to a gal like Allene is a little like being the object in a knife-throwing act at the circus. So if you and Brock are planning a surprise for her—well, I just hope it's one that will set her back on her heels, but good!"

She looked up at Brock, all smiling, wide-eyed innocence, and added kindly, "Allene can be quite a witch when she sets her mind to it, but I'm sure you already have learned that, darling."

She gave them a little airy wave of a jeweled hand and allowed herself to be steered back to her party and their table.

Nora lifted her head stubbornly and walked out. On the sidewalk, Brock said harshly "I'll drive you home, of course."

They drove the distance in silence, with Brock staring straight ahead of him, his eyes on the road, his hands gripping the wheel tightly. When they had reached the tall, stately old house tucked in between the two tall buildings, he followed her up the steps and into the house, where Nora turned on him sharply.

"Good night, Brock," she said curtly. "It's been no fun at all, and thank you for making a mess of my affairs."

"I'm terribly sorry."

"Good night!" Nora repeated distinctly, and turned away.

After a moment, Brock turned and walked out.

Nora dropped down on the bottom step of the stairs and put her face in her hands and knew a deep and very real sickness that was almost as much physical as it was mental.

She did not hear the door open, but she glanced up as she heard a burst of gay laughter. She looked straight into Jay's white, angry face—and knew that Jay had seen Brock leaving.

For a moment there was a taut silence.

The girls were brightly interested. Jay was glowering at her accusingly. And suddenly she felt an absurd desire to laugh.

"Isn't it funny?" she stammered, and heard the hysterical note in her voice.

She heard one of the girls say with friendly curiosity, "Drunk?"

She gasped and fought the hysteria that was bubbling in her throat, as she heard Jay say grimly, "I don't think so!" as he bent above her, sniffing deliberately. She drew sharply away from him, her anger mastering the hysteria for just a moment.

"Don't be insulting," she flung at them furiously.

"She's not drunk," Jay informed the girls, "just temporarily out of her mind. At least I *hope* it's temporary. You girls scoot on to bed; tomorrow's a working day. I'll take care of her."

Susan hesitated at the foot of the stairs, lively curiosity in her eyes as she studied Nora.

"You're sure there's nothing we can do?" she asked Jay.

"Quite sure," Jay said grimly, and put his hand under Nora's arm and hoisted her unceremoniously to her feet.

"It must have been quite a party," Lucy commented as she followed Susan up the stairs.

Nora tried to wrench herself free of Jay, sputtering with helpless fury, but Jay propelled her down the hall to the kitchen and there deposited her unceremoniously on a chair.

"So you couldn't keep away from the big lug, eh?" he growled as he started making coffee.

Nora was still fighting against the idiotic hysteria that had flooded her when she had realized that Jay, arriving, had met Brock, departing from what must have seemed a clandestine date.

"I don't know what you mean." She clamped her lips shut, fighting to steady her voice.

Busy with the coffee, Jay glanced over his shoulder at her, and his look was contemptuously cold.

"Like heck you don't!" he growled. "If there's anything in this world I loathe it's a two-timing female!"

"If you'd only let me explain!"

"I'm all ears!"

"And prepared to call me a liar before I even start."

"Well, you've got to admit the circumstantial evidence is pretty strong. I overtook you just as you were about to jump blithely in his car the very minute his prospective ball-and-chain left on her way to New York; and now while she is still in New York, you have been out dining and dancing with him."

"And is that a crime?"

"Well, you'll have to admit it's not in the very best taste—the ex-boy friend dating the ex-girl friend the minute his affianced bride's back is turned."

"But it wasn't like that at all," she protested hotly, and did not realize even in that moment how desperately important it was to make him understand. "I was—well, I was lonely. I decided to have dinner out; and Luigi's is one of the few places I knew where I wouldn't be conspicuous dining alone. Lots of business women, widows, women who live alone go there. And—well, then Brock came in."

"Just happened along by accident, and said, 'Well, well, long time no see—mind if I join you'? How did he know you were there?"

Color poured into Nora's eyes and she could not go on meeting his eyes.

"Luigi telephoned him after I got there," she admitted huskily.

Jay's eyebrows went up.

"At your instructions, I'm sure."

"Of course not! Brock had left instructions there that if I came in alone, they were to telephone him."

"Well, now, that was downright neighborly of him, wasn't it? He was going to sit right by his telephone every evening waiting for a call from Luigi. Suppose you hadn't gone in? Your pal would have spent a lot of lonely evenings waiting by the telephone, wouldn't he?"

Nora said huskily, "You think I called Brock—"

"Or that he called you and you met at Luigi's by appointment. What else would anyone think?"

His tone stung her so that she rose to her feet, eyes blazing.

"I don't care one tinker's dam for what you or anyone else thinks," she blazed at him furiously. "What business is it of yours, anyway? Who asked you to stick your nose into my affairs?"

"Nobody," Jay answered curtly. "But nobody! I was just fool enough to think that I was in love with you and wanted to look after you—which will probably give you many a hearty laugh in years to come! But it's true. I not only admired you; I respected you for being such a straightforward, honest person who'd never stoop to two-timing."

"I hate that word!"

"I don't doubt that you do. The truth always hurts, doesn't it?"

Nora stood very still for a moment, hands clenched tightly at her sides, her head high, bright spots of color in her cheeks.

"Aren't you making a mountain out of a molehill?" she asked after a moment. "After all, I went out to dinner; quite by accident, an old friend happened in; we had dinner together and he brought me home. Would you mind pointing out to me just where I have fallen so far in your estimation?"

Jay looked her over, his jaw grim and hard.

"By accident?"

"So far as I was concerned, it *was* by accident," she insisted.

"And when he arrived, you couldn't just get up and walk out and leave him standing there with egg on his face?"

"I didn't think of that," she stammered, and added defensively, "I had just ordered my dinner, and it had been served, and I was hungry."

It sounded pitifully foolish even in her own ears. But it was true. It hadn't occurred to her just to get up and walk out on Brock, although now she knew that was what she should have done. And then Nancy Sutherland and her party wouldn't have seen them together.

She dropped down at the table, rested her elbows on the table edge and put her face in her hands.

"Oh, Jay, I've been such a fool!" she wailed.

"I'll buy that!" Jay told her grimly, without the slightest softening of his voice or warming of his cold eyes as he brought cups from the pantry and poured two steaming cups of coffee. "Here, drink this."

She looked up at him miserably.

"I haven't told you all of it," she confessed humbly.

Jay scowled at her. "There's more?"

She nodded and told him of Nancy's bright malice when she had seen her with Brock, and Jay lit a cigarette and let his coffee cool as he studied her.

"And this Nancy gal will break her neck to tell the fair Allene that while the cat's been away the pet mouse has been scampering out of bounds. Pretty!" he commented acidly.

"And Allene will very likely cancel out on all Belloti's plans for her wedding and I'll be fired in disgrace."

Jay nodded slowly, his brows furrowed.

"Could be," he agreed thoughtfully.

Nora wailed suddenly, like a frightened child, "Oh, Jay, what am I going to do?"

Jay studied her without sympathy.

"I'd suggest you keep away from Tall, Dark and Loathesome, and pray," he said grimly, "that Nancy won't spill the beans!"

Nora shook her head.

"I know Nancy. She's not one to keep a secret!"

"So in future the smart thing for you to do is not to provide her with any secrets, isn't it?"

She stood up, thrust the untouched coffee aside, and looked down at him where he still sat, his cigarette trailing a thin cloud of blue smoke between them.

"My conscience," she told him distinctly, "is quite clear! I have done nothing to be ashamed of."

"You know, of course," Jay ignored her words, spoke as though he had not even heard, "that he'll never marry you, even if Allene bounces him?"

"Oh, yes, he would!" Nora flashed hotly. "In fact, that was why he wanted to see me tonight: to tell me that he realizes his engagement to Allene is all a mistake and if I'll marry him, he'll break with her."

Jay's eyes held a sardonic amusement that was like a slap.

"You know he was lying—or you're not as smart as I thought you were."

Nora said through her teeth, "Apparently I'm not a good many things you once thought I was!"

And Jay said an unforgivable thing: "I'll buy that!"

Nora caught her breath as though he had slapped her and turned and went out of the kitchen and up the stairs.

12

THE WHOLE miserable evening had been a disaster. All she had had in mind when she had decided to have dinner at Luigi's was to be back for a little while in once familiar scenes; to get her mind away from Belloti's and the many tiresome, tedious problems that clogged her days. Not even now would she admit that one reason she had wanted so much to get out of the house tonight had been because Jay and his crew-cut friend and the two girls had so obviously been headed for a gay evening and she had been jealous.

She fell asleep at last from sheer mental exhaustion and awoke late. She had to hurry greatly to get dressed and ready for work, and when she came running out of the house, breathless for fear she had missed the bus that, with any luck, would get her to Belloti's by a quarter of nine, Jay was waiting in the drive for her.

He swung open the car door for her and said brusquely,

"Make it snappy. We'll just make it if we can get all the traffic lights in our favor. What a hope!"

Nora scrambled into the car, slammed the door and turned gratefully to him.

"Thanks for waiting for me, Jay," she said warmly.

"Save the thanks. I was late myself," he said curtly. "I should never drink coffee late at night. Always makes me oversleep."

He slid the car into the town-bound traffic, and from then on, his attention was confined to his driving, and there was no conversation between them until they reached the parking lot with two minutes to spare. They reached Belloti's just as the big bell rang, and they smiled at each other like breathless schoolchildren who have just missed being tardy!

"Made it!" was all Jay said as, with a wave of the hand, he moved off to the elevator that would take him straight to the sixth floor, while Nora turned to the one that was an express to the fourth floor.

She was still breathing a little fast when she reached her office, but at least she was on time.

She was immediately caught up in her various duties, and it was lunch time before she realized it. There was time only for a hurried rush to the employees' cafeteria, because she had an appointment at one-thirty with a bride-to-be who was "being difficult" about her final fittings.

As she reached a table with her tray, Connie Terrell came swiftly to sit with her. But Connie was so changed that it was a moment before Nora could recognize her. Connie had a strained, haggard look that made her plain face downright homely; and there was a desolate look in her eyes that made Nora forget that she was hungry.

"Why, Connie," she gasped, "what's wrong?"

"Everything!" said Connie desolately, and swallowed a sob. "I won't be able to have my dress, Nora. I've got to give it up."

"Why, Connie?"

Connie fought tears for a moment, set her teeth hard

in her lower lip and managed to say huskily, "It's Pop. He had a bad fall at the plant, and he needs an operation, and the family will need what I've saved. So I can't have the dress."

"Oh, but, Connie, it's almost finished. I saw it in the workroom yesterday, and it's lovely."

Connie shook her head, and two tears spilled out, sliding down her haggard young face.

"I know, Nora. Oh, I never wanted anything so much in all my life. But how'd I feel to know my family was maybe starving just so I could prance around in a custom-made wedding gown?" she stammered. "Pop can have surgery at the charity hospital. We've never accepted charity before, but I guess there always has to be a first time. But it takes a lot of food for a big family like ours— and rent—and my salary won't cover it. No, Nora, I stayed awake all night trying to find some other way. But now I know it would be the most wicked thing in the world for me to use that money for a dress like that. So will you please tell them to cancel it? It's such a lovely dress— maybe they can alter it for somebody else—or even put it in the Budget Shop or the Fashion Fourth." She got to her feet and went off, almost running, and Nora saw her shoulders quivering as she fought the bitter tears that were sliding down her face.

Nora stared after her, and then sat for a moment, stunned. Nora felt almost as though she herself had been denied some precious, cherished thing, and when she went back to her office, her thoughts were still busy with the problem. But by closing time, she was as far from a solution as she had been at the first moment Connie had blurted out her news.

She came out of the employees' entrance, trying to assure herself that she was not looking for Jay nor disappointed when she did not see him. Someone spoke her name, and she turned to find a group of women smiling anxiously at her.

"You're Miss Robinson, from the Bridal Shop," said the elderly, gray-haired woman who seemed to be the spokesman for the group of four women. "We'd like to talk to you if we may. If you aren't busy, maybe you'd have dinner with us so we can talk comfortably."

Puzzled, Nora said, "I'm not busy, but—"

The woman's thin, tired face was touched with a smile.

"You're wondering what in Sam Hill a bunch of old biddies like us want to talk about with a Bridal Consultant," she said. Nora laughed and shook her head, and the woman went on, "We're friends of Connie Terrell. I'm her supervisor—name's Mary Jordan. This is Ellen Smith, Marcia Sutphen, and Louise Lee. We've all known Connie since she first came to Belloti's, and we're very fond of her. We know she's had to cancel her wedding dress, and we thought maybe there might be something we could do, if we could talk about it with you."

"Well, indeed you can," Nora agreed eagerly. "And I'd love to have dinner with you and see what we could work out."

Mary nodded in satisfaction to the others.

"See? Connie said she was reg'lar! Come on, girls." She led the way to a small, clean café not far from the store, and when they were settled, she leaned across the table toward Nora. "Of course, Miss Robinson, we all thought Connie was foolish to put her whole life's savings into a wedding dress she'd wear just once. But when we realized how much it meant to her, we didn't argue with her. Connie's a good kid, one of the best. Works her head off, and is so devoted to that family of hers that it never makes any difference to her how shabbily she has to dress, or how many times she has to have her shoes half-soled, so long as that bunch of kids is dressed decently for school and Sunday school. We thought she just *ought* to have this one perfect thing she's always wanted—a pretty wedding to remember and a beautiful dress. So we're going to try to raise the money to pay for the dress. You haven't told the Shop to cancel it, have you?" she finished in sudden alarm.

"Oh, no," Nora admitted. "It will be ready within a week, and to cancel it now—"

"Well, don't!" Mary said briskly. "I feel sure that if we canvass the whole basement, everybody who knows Connie will be glad to contribute a dollar or more, and we can scrape up the whole amount."

"Why, that's wonderful!" Nora glowed happily. "I'd like to contribute ten dollars to start the fund off. But will Connie be embarrassed?"

"Get her feelings hurt, you mean?" Mary sniffed disdainfully. "Well, what if she does? A custom-made gown that she's wanted since she was a child ought to soothe a lot of hurt feelings. And I don't think Connie will feel hurt, because she'll know that we did it because we love her. And nobody can have her feelings hurt by people who love them, now can she? It would be like—oh, like refusing to accept a Christmas gift!"

"It'll be a wedding present!" said one of the women happily. "And she'd never be able to refuse that! She knows everybody in the whole basement has been contributing to a wedding present for her, so we'll just put the whole business into the dress!"

Nora looked about the group: four women in their late fifties or early sixties, who she knew must have been working for Belloti's for many years, because Belloti's rarely employed a saleswoman who was over forty. Tired-looking women, who had many financial responsibilities and family problems, yet they were as excited as a group of young girls at the prospect of seeing Connie's dream fulfilled.

"Connie's a very lucky girl to have such wonderful friends," she said warmly.

"Oh, well, Connie's a fine girl," Mary Jordan dismissed that airily. "Now what we've got to decide is how we're going to give Connie the dress, and see to it she has a pretty wedding to go with it. Anybody have any ideas?"

"Oh, let me give her the wedding itself," suggested Nora eagerly, "At my home! I've had a lot of dealings with florists around town, setting up decorations for some of the weddings the Shop has handled, and I'll take care of all that. We could let the whole thing be a surprise for

Connie. Suppose I invite her and Hank to dinner that night. And then when she gets there everything will be ready. How does that sound?"

The four women's glowing faces and their eager assent was proof that it sounded very good to them.

"I'll arrange for a minister of Connie's own faith. Do you suppose there is one she would prefer? Someone in her own church?" asked Nora eagerly.

"She and Hank have arranged with the minister of her church, I think," said Mary, and raised her eyebrows questioningly at the others.

Ellen Smith nodded. "Preacher Singleton, of the Far Hills Baptist, the church Connie has attended since she was a kid," she announced. "I'll talk to him, if you like, Miss Robinson. He's my pastor, too."

"Oh, wonderful!" said Nora eagerly, and added, "Now how are we going to arrange for Hank to be on hand with a marriage license ready?"

Mary laughed. "Oh, that's my job. I know Hank well. He's *almost* good enough for Connie, which shows you how well I like him."

"Well, then." Nora beamed joyously at them, and laughed. "Oh, it's going to be so wonderful to see Connie's face when she knows what we have planned for her."

"There's just one thing we have to be careful about," Mary warned them, "and that's to be sure Connie knows nothing about what we are planning. It's to be a complete surprise. Agreed?"

"Oh, of course," the others chorused gaily. They smiled at each other, and Nora felt her eyes mist a little as she looked at the happiness glowing in their eyes.

They all fell to planning and discussing, and it was an hour or more before they finished dinner and came out into the golden afterglow of the long twilight.

"I'll have to admit, Miss Robinson—" Mary began, but Nora put out her hand swiftly and laid it on Mary's.

"Oh, please, not Miss Robinson. I'm Nora to my friends," she said eagerly, and looked about the group. "And I'm envious of Connie having such wonderful friends. I hope you're going to be my friends, too!"

Mary studied her curiously even as she smiled.

"Well, that's for sure, Nora," she said happily. "I'm surprised, I have to admit. I've always felt the Bridal Shop was made up of a rather snooty bunch; I'm glad to find out that there is at least one like you."

"Oh, we're all of us intensely human, I assure you." She laughed. "We get terribly involved with some of our clients, and they *do* keep us on the run. But when we get someone like Connie—"

"And I'll bet that doesn't happen often," Mary commented dryly, but she was smiling so there was no sting in the words.

"Well, no, it doesn't," Nora had to admit ruefully. "But if you could see how everybody from the designer right to the newest and most awkward sewing girl has been determined that Connie's should be a really fabulous frock, you'd believe that we *are* human!"

"Well, as I was going to say, Nora, I'll have to admit that this has all taken a vast load off my mind." Mary smiled at her. "I've felt as low as Connie ever since she told me this morning she was going to have to give up her dress. That girl has her heart set on one lovely, never-to-be-forgotten hour in her life—and the thought that she was going to have to give it up and just be married in some old thing—"

She blinked rapidly and managed a smile that was somewhat tremulous as she and the others bade Nora good night and set off for their bus.

13

Dusk was tempering the afterglow when she reached the steps in front of her home, and she went up the steps and along the walk, smiling reminiscently, absorbed in her thoughts of Connie and her plans for the wedding.

She let herself into the house just as Jay started down the stairs, and for a moment he paused and eyed her sharply.

"Aren't you a bit late?" he growled.

But Nora was locked fast in her thoughts of Connie and for the moment could not remember that she and Jay had quarreled. She faced him radiantly, eyes shining.

"Oh, Jay, the most wonderful thing has happened!" she caroled. "Connie and Hank are going to be married *here*. She won't have to give up her cherished dream of a wedding out of a story-book, after all. Isn't that wonderful?"

Puzzled, but with relief showing in his eyes, Jay came on down the stairs and stood looking down at her.

"Well, fill me in," he suggested. "I didn't know there was any danger of her not being allowed to squander her life's savings."

Swiftly, still forgetting that last night she and Jay had quarreled furiously, Nora told him about her talk with Connie at lunch and then the meeting with the four middle-aged supervisors. And as she raced on, cheeks flushed, eyes aglow, Jay watched her with a curious intentness, not interrupting. When she had finished, he nodded.

"Your clients do seem to be slipping out from under your control, don't they?" he drawled, apparently not at all touched by her breathless excitement. "I don't wonder you're delighted at being able to keep Connie from canceling her order."

Nora stepped back as though he had slapped her, and some of the brightness vanished from her face as she stiffened.

"That was a rotten thing to say!" she flung at him furiously.

Jay had the grace to look faintly ashamed.

"I know it was. Could I take it back?" he asked awkwardly.

Nora nodded, a little of her brightness returning.

"I wish you would," she told him. "I'm so happy and so excited I don't want to quarrel with anybody tonight."

"Not even me?"

Her smile was faint, cool.

"Not even with you," she repeated, and rushed on eagerly. "Oh, Jay, if you could have seen those women! They were so anxious to save Connie's dream dress, and so delighted when I said we'd have the wedding here and I'd provide the flowers and all decorations—and refreshments, too!"

"Hi, now, wait a minute!" Jay protested. "That could run into quite an expense."

"Oh, I don't care!" Nora beamed recklessly. "I want this wedding to be as perfect as Connie's dreams. And it's going to be, as far as I can manage it."

Jay was thoughtful.

"Count me in, too," he told her. And before she could do more than blink, he went on swiftly, "Of course you know what a perfectly swell 'human interest' story this would make for the newspapers. Be swell publicity for the Bridal Shop and Belloti's, too, and probably garner all sorts of loot for the happy couple."

"Oh, no," Nora protested swiftly. "It would humiliate Connie to tears, and it wouldn't be good for Hank. His firm might take a dim view of their 'leg man' getting himself married in a sort of three-ring circus affair! We're going to have trouble enough getting Connie to accept the dress! She has a great deal of pride."

Jay nodded thoughtfully, his eyes still on Nora's face with that odd, speculative look.

"That figures," he agreed. "But it would make a whale of a story."

"I don't think Belloti's would like it, either," Nora insisted.

Jay grinned. "Well, it *would* sort of emphasize the fact that they overcharge their hired hands as much as they do the local citizenry," he admitted, and added before she could take offense, "Well, count me in. I'll provide the refreshments out of my own little pocket—with an 'assist' here and there from the catering establishments that owe me a few favors."

Susan and Lucy were coming down the stairs, and Susan called gaily, "Is this a private fight or may we have an invitation to join in?"

Nora turned eagerly and lifted a laughing face toward the two girls.

"How'd you like to be bridesmaids at a wedding here a week from now?" she demanded.

"A wedding?" Susan and Lucy exchanged swift glances, and Susan added, "That would depend on whose wedding. Yours and Jay's? That we wouldn't like!"

Nora laughed and carefully did not look at Jay, who was watching her unsmilingly.

"Oh, goodness, no," she laughed. "It's a girl from the store."

Swiftly she explained, and the two girls caught fire from her own enthusiasm.

"Hi, that sounds like fun," said Susan eagerly. "But are you sure she won't want her own friends in her wedding party?"

"Oh, it's going to be a surprise!" Nora answered.

"For her? Or for the groom?" Susan wanted to know blandly.

"For her, silly! The groom will know all about it, because he's got to get the license," Nora explained, her voice caught with laughter. "I'm inviting them here for dinner; and once they are here, you and Lucy and I will whisk her off upstairs and get her into the wedding gown. Then you can lead the way downstairs, while somebody sings 'Oh, Promise Me' or something. You see? She'll be overcome with surprise—"

"That she will," Susan agreed. "But if she really wants to marry the guy, who are Lucy and I to stop her? We'll be bridesmaids, and give her a solid silver lemon fork for a wedding present."

"Oh, thanks, that's lovely of you!" Nora beamed at them. "She's dreamed about this wedding for so long; it's the one moment in her life when she can count on being really *beautiful*. And she will be, because it's a heavenly frock and wickedly becoming."

"And I suppose the groom-to-be will be stunned with her loveliness and feel he's marrying a glamorous stranger," Lucy suggested.

Jay said sharply, "The guy's crazy about her. She's always been beautiful to him, and she will be no different no matter how you dress her up—to him, anyway. He's always seen her through the eyes of his love, and nothing could beautify a girl any more."

The three girls were staring at him, wide-eyed.

"Well, forevermore!" murmured Lucy, slightly awed by the vehemence of his tone.

Jay grinned wryly. "So bear that in mind, my fine-feathered friends," he warned them. "The next time somebody tries to talk you into spending a month's salary to 'glamorize' yourself for some poor boob, just remember; if he's in love with you, it's an unnecessary waste of money; and if he isn't, then it's an even more unnecessary waste."

The three girls eyed him and then exchanged significant glances.

"Maybe I'm wrong," drawled Lucy after a moment, "but I somehow get the idea this fellow is against us gals."

Nora laughed and shook her head. "He's not against us gals. He just doesn't think very highly of the Bridal Shop and bridal consultants and fancy wedding gowns."

"Oh, well, he's never been a bride." Lucy laughed, her eyes warm and tender on Jay. "You'll see. When some smart gal throws a lasso over him, he'll be so groggy he won't know what hit him."

She came on down the stairs and tucked her hand possessively through Jay's arm and smiled up at him tenderly.

"Well, shall we go? We're to meet Bill at the Glass House, remember?" she reminded him.

Nora felt a small, cold hand close over her eager heart and could not keep a smile pinned to her face as she stepped back and let Susan join Lucy and Jay.

As they turned toward the door, Jay hesitated and asked, "Won't you join us, Nora? We'd love to have you, wouldn't we, girls?"

Nora saw the slight stiffening of Lucy's body before she turned her head, eyed Nora without warmth and said politely, "Why, yes, of course we would."

And in a voice just as devoid of warmth but just as polite, Susan said, "Oh, yes, do, Nora."

"Thanks, but I've already had dinner," Nora answered. "Nice of you to ask me, though. Some other time, perhaps."

"Of course, any time," said Jay, and allowed himself to be drawn out of the house by the two girls, one on either arm.

Nora watched them go, listened to the sound of his car and felt the bright wings of her spirits droop as she turned and went on up the stairs to her own room.

There was a little sheaf of mail on the bedside table, and she riffled through it, dropping unopened into the wastebasket the circulars, wincing a little as she saw the telltale envelopes of bills. At the bottom of the sheaf there was a letter from her mother with a Palm Beach postmark.

She waited to open it until she had changed from her office dress to a housecoat and slippers. Then she curled up on the wide windowseat, beside the open window, and slit the envelope.

But before she had finished reading the first page she was sitting bolt upright, her eyes wide, racing down the page, trying to take it all in. *Her mother had married again!*

She put down the letter and stared straight before her. There was no real reason, she tried to tell herself, that she should be so utterly dumbfounded. After all, Celia was still a lovely woman, and in her mid-forties. And there was nothing remarkable about the fact that she had met a man who thought so, too. It was just that the news had come without the slightest warning. Celia hadn't even mentioned the man in her recent letters. Nora took up the letter and read it again, this time more carefully. The man's name, Gordon MacFarlaine, was not unfamiliar, she had read it in the newspaper. He was very wealthy; he was a long-time widower; he was in his sixties.

She was glad for her mother, if that was what her mother wanted. But as she thought of her father, a desolate feeling crept over her. She had never felt so alone, so forlorn in all her life.

"Aunt Alicia was dreadfully upset," Celia had written gaily. "I can't think why—she couldn't possibly have wanted Gordy for herself, now could she? Anyway, Precious, we are as wildly happy as a couple of children. We're sailing for Europe for a few months, and as soon as we get back, you must do something about the house. Sell it, if you like and come to visit us in New York and let me help you find a nice, suitable young man."

Nora put down the letter and ran her fingers through her tumbled curls, managing a small, rueful laugh. It was good to know her mother was happy; that she would be able to enjoy even more luxury and extravagance than her first husband had been able to give her.

She had never felt so surrounded by wedding talk in her life, she told herself forlornly. Allene and Brock; Penny and Tommy; Hank and Connie; and now her mother.

She was still trying to lever herself out of the depths of

her gloom when there was a gentle knock at the door, and Emma put her head inside to say, "There's a young lady waiting to see you downstairs, Miss Nora."

"Only she's not downstairs any longer," said Allene Larrimore's cool voice behind Emma, who turned, startled.

"Oh, but, miss, I asked you—" she stammered.

Allene brushed past her contemptuously.

"Run along, for heaven's sake," she snapped at Emma, her eyes cool and hostile on Nora's startled face. "This is a personal matter, and we don't need an audience."

She closed the door in Emma's face and stood, her arms folded, eyeing Nora with an ugly scrutiny.

"Surprised to see me?" she asked crisply.

"Well, I expected to see you at the shop in a day or so," Nora answered as coolly, "but I'm a little surprised to see you here."

"The moment Nancy telephoned me I took the first flight out of New York," Allene told her, and her lips thinned in an entirely mirthless smile. "I didn't even have time to buy you a present to bring home with me, though I'm sure I can pick up a healthy, live rattlesnake somewhere in these parts and have it suitably gift-wrapped for you."

"So?" Nora's chin tilted a little.

"So I'm warning you to keep your paws off my man," Allene said curtly. "I suppose you thought you might get him back while I was out of town."

"I don't *want* him."

"Oh, no, you don't!" sneered Allene, flinging the lie in her teeth. "You'd marry him in a flash if you could afford him; but since you can't I'm warning you to let him alone. No more sneaking off to dinner with him at Luigi's—no more secret dates with him."

"I don't suppose it would do a bit of good to tell you that we met entirely by accident—" Nora began. Then she remembered Luigi had telephoned Brock, and her voice trailed off to a shamed silence.

"You don't really expect me to believe that, do you?"

Allene answered harshly. "I hope you don't, because it's as feeble a lie as I ever heard. You may as well face up to the fact that I have my Indian sign on Brock and I am not even thinking about letting you have him back."

"Oh," said Nora, and could not quite keep the relief out of her voice, "then you're going on with your plans for your wedding?"

Allene's airy brows went up a little.

"And why wouldn't I?" she demanded. "Do you really think I'd stop now? I never heard of anything so silly. Do you think for a moment that I would break off my engagement to Brock just because he was seen dining with you while I was out of town? You really *are* a fool, Nora! I've never kidded myself about Brock for so much as a moment. I know perfectly well that he is no more in love with me than I am with him. But believe it or not, we have a lot to give each other. I can give him the wealth that he craves; he can give me a securely established social position. Of course we'll probably fight like cats and dogs, but so what? We'll each have what we want, and I imagine ours will be about as happy a marriage as any in our set."

"I hope so," Nora said and could not quite keep the distaste out of her voice. She added frankly, "I'm awfully relieved, Allene, that you aren't canceling your order at the shop. With everything just about ready to be delivered, to have you suddenly change your mind would —well, it would make things pretty unpleasant for me, because I'm sure you'd be happy to explain to Mrs. Anstruthers just why you were canceling."

Allene studied her curiously for a moment, her brows drawn together in a frown of concentration.

"There *is* that, of course," she mused aloud, following a thought that had obviously not occurred to her until now. "It would be even more fun than making you a present of a gift-wrapped rattlesnake! I'd love to see Mrs. Anstruthers' face if Mother and I told her we were canceling thousands of dollars worth of wedding plans just because *you* were trying to get Brock away from me. It's a tempting thought, I admit."

Nora held her breath and wondered why she had been fool enough to blurt out her fears. She waited, watching Allene fearfully, and then Allene laughed.

"It's a tempting thought," she admitted, "but I prefer to go on and marry Brock just as planned. The wedding preparations are really lush, and I'd hate to give them up. It's going to be far and away the most fashionable wedding Belloti's has staged in years. And Belloti's stages all the best ones. So I'm marrying Brock as planned. And you're to keep away from him, do you understand?"

Nora was drawn to her full height, her eyes blazing with outrage.

"It will be a pleasure!" she said hotly.

Allene's eyes raked her from head to foot, then dismissed her contemptuously as she opened the door and went out.

14

WHEN NORA came down the stairs the following morning, Jay was waiting for her, the morning paper in his hands. He looked up at her as she reached the foot of the steps.

"Emma says we can have coffee before we leave, and I think you'd better have a cup before you see this," he told her, and there was a touch of grimness in his voice. He marched her back to the kitchen, where Emma greeted them with a pleasant good morning and two cups of steaming coffee.

"But what *is* it?" Nora asked, bewildered.

"Drink your orange juice and your coffee and brace

yourself," Jay insisted, holding the folded paper away from her.

"If it's anything about Allene Larrimore and Brock Neilson—" she began.

Jay scowled at her.

"It isn't. Why should you think it might be?" he demanded.

Nora sipped her orange juice and said quietly, "She was here last night, to apologize for not bringing me a present from New York."

Jay murmured something under his breath that made Emma give him a startled glance.

"Neighborly of her, I must say," Jay commented dryly. "Like maybe a cancelation of all the 'pretties' she had ordered for her wedding?"

A gleam of laughter showed briefly in Nora's eyes.

"Oh, no, she had in mind a gift-wrapped rattlesnake."

Jay's brows went up and his eyes chilled.

"A thought that sounds quite worthy of the gal," he drawled. "Did you thank her politely? And then I suppose she canceled—"

Nora shook her head.

"Oh, no, the marriage will take place as scheduled, with all the 'pretties'."

Jay shook his head.

"Women!" he murmured. "Well, if you've finished your coffee, I suppose you may as well see this."

He unfolded the paper before her, and there on the front page were headlines topping two pictures: one of Penny Livingston, a posed studio portrait, and one of Tommy Parker. The headlines announced that at an early hour that morning, Tommy Parker's car had smashed. And in the wreckage was not only Tommy but also a young woman from a south side address, at the edge of an unsavory neighborhood. Both were critically injured but still alive when rushed to the hospital. Both had a good chance of surviving. Though the account was circumspect, carefully written, there was an inescapable odor of scandal about it.

Jay watched Nora's wide eyes as they raced through the brief but damning account. When she looked up at him, she saw something very like compassion in his eyes.

"So now, of course, you've lost Penny," Jay pointed out. "Naturally, she won't go on with her plans to marry him now. Not when he could indulge in an escapade with a woman of that type just a week or two before the wedding."

"Poor Penny!" Nora murmured.

Jay said quietly at last, "Well, shall we hop on our horses and head for the pass, pal?"

Nora looked up at him and then again at the paper and stood up.

"I—yes, of course," she stammered, and added foolishly, "I forgot to tell you. Rather, I didn't have a chance. I had a letter from Mother last night."

"Oh?" Jay's interest was obviously so mild as to be scarcely polite as they hurried out of the house and to his car. "I hope she is well."

"Oh, I'm sure she is," Nora told him. "She's on her honeymoon."

Jay stared at her, slack-jawed.

"She's what?"

Nora nodded. "That's right. She has just been married and is about to sail for Europe aboard her new husband's yacht."

Jay was silent, concentrating, as he slid the car out of the drive and into the thickening stream of rush-hour traffic toward town.

"She seems quite happy," Nora contributed after a moment.

"And how do you feel about it?"

"Oh, I'm glad for her, of course."

Jay relaxed visibly.

"Then that's all right," he said as though she had taken quite a burden off his mind. "I have never in all my life seen anything like it. A man goes around minding his own business, scarcely ever thinking about the allegedly holy bonds of matrimony—and then suddenly he's up to his ears in chatter about nothing else!"

Nora tilted her chin defiantly and her eyes chilled.

"I'm sorry you find me so boring," she flashed at him hotly.

"Not you, baby, but all this wedding business. I feel I'm smothering in a sea of whipped cream and tulle and creamed chicken and champagne."

"I feel a little that way myself," Nora confessed, as though ashamed of the confession. "Honestly, I never dreamed there could be so much fuss and feathers about two people just deciding they'd like to be married. When it comes time for me, I'm simply going hand in hand with my man right down to the Marriage License Bureau and get it over with!"

Jay laughed shortly. "I'll bet!" he derided. "You'll probably insist on having everything the Larrimore dame has—except, of course, the man."

"Whom I don't want, never did—"

"Never?"

"Oh, well." There was a color in Nora's face, and her eyes would not quite meet his. "There *was* a time when I thought he was pretty special. But that was before I really knew him at all."

"And now?" Jay probed, as the car idled for a moment waiting for the traffic light to change.

"And now Allene is more than welcome to him," Nora said quietly, but with such conviction that, as the light changed, Jay glanced at her swiftly with a smile more friendly than any he had given her in the last few days.

"Now you're getting some sense," he said and his tone added that he thought it was high time.

They reached Bellotti's and separated with friendly smiles, and Nora hurried up to her office, feeling gay and light-hearted, to face the usual hectic day. . . .

"Penny," said Mrs. Livingston gently.

Penny, huddled beside the bed where Tommy lay, her hands closed tightly about his that lay laxly on the covers, did not look up. Her eyes were riveted on Tommy's face, all that she could see of it beneath the turban-like bandages about his head.

"Penny, dear," Mrs. Livingston said again, her eyes sick with pity for the girl, as she put out a gentle hand and laid it on the girl's shoulder. "Penny, child, look at me."

Awkwardly Penny turned her white face up to her grandmother and then back again so that she could go on looking at Tommy. She bent until her warm lips were against his ear, and her murmuring resumed; the murmuring she had been pouring into his unconscious ears since they had brought him back here from the operating room.

"Tommy! Tommy." Her soft voice ached with anguished love. "Tommy, listen to me, honey. Tommy, it's Penny! You're not going to try to get away from me, are you, Tommy? Oh, that would be a dirty trick. And it wouldn't do you any good, because wherever you go I'll follow you. You hear me, Tommy? We're a team! You can't run out on me, Tommy. I won't let you."

Mrs. Livingston felt that if she had to listen to that soft, murmuring voice another hour, she would go to pieces. She put her arm about the girl's shoulders and rested her cheek against the white, strained face.

"Precious, he can't hear you," she said thickly.

But Penny pulled away from the loving arms.

"How do we know he can't?" she protested huskily. He's breathing."

"And he's going to live, Penny darling. Remember the doctors said so?" Mrs. Livingston said huskily. "But come away now, darling, and rest. You can't help him."

"He'll know I'm here, and that will help him."

"Dearest, Tommy's father wants to see you," Mrs. Livingston urged. "You can come back here as soon as you have talked to him."

Reluctantly, wincing a little as her muscles, cramped by her long vigil, protested against the movement, Penny managed to stand up. But before she left the bedside, she bent low once more, her lips touching his ear.

"You wait right here, Tommy," she told him huskily. "I'll be right back."

She turned at the door, glanced back at the still, heavily bandaged figure and then, drawing a deep, hard breath, let herself be guided out of the room and down the corridor to where a small group of people stood at the doorway of a reception room.

Mr. and Mrs. Parker came swiftly to meet her, their faces white and strained, their eyes dark with worry. Mrs. Parker put out her arms, but Penny side-stepped with a little flutter of her hands.

"Don't touch me," she pleaded unsteadily. "I'll fall apart if you do."

"Penny darling, I've just talked to the young woman who was with Tommy when the accident happened," said Mr. Parker.

"Why?" asked Penny, puzzled. "What's she got to do with all this?"

"Dear child, she was with Tommy when the accident happened." Mr. Parker's voice broke slightly, but he went on swiftly, "Tommy wasn't dating her."

Penny stared at him as though he had made the most absurd remark on record.

"Well, of course he wasn't! Tommy *wouldn't.*"

Such simple faith seemed to the three older people almost frightening. Mr. Parker went on:

"Seems after he took you home last night—this morning—whenever it was, Tommy stopped at a drive-in for a hamburger."

"A hot dog," Penny corrected him. "Tommy hates hamburgers."

Mr. Parker nodded. "Anyway, this girl served him. She admired his car; she said something about being off duty and having to fight her way to the South Side on a bus and walk two blocks along a dark street. There have been some unpleasant happenings in that neighborhood."

"So Tommy offered to drive her home," Penny finished

for him, and seemed bewildered that he had found it necessary to make such an investigation. "What else would Tommy do, in a case like that?"

"You don't mind the scandal?" Mrs. Parker asked.

Penny looked from one to the other of the older people, and her brows drew together in a puzzled frown.

"Scandal?" she repeated as though she had never heard the word before and wasn't at all sure of its meaning.

"Well, an accident, very late at night, to a young man engaged to be married very soon and a young woman—" Mr. Parker struggled to make himself plain, and felt his words dropping into silence beneath the clear if somewhat puzzled glance that Penny was giving him.

"Scandal? Because Tommy gave a lift to a girl who'd been running her feet off all evening serving food in a drive-in, and was scared to walk two blocks alone at that time of night? What's there to make a scandal about?"

Mr. Parker said softly, "You're quite a girl, Penny. And forgive me."

Bewildered, Penny looked from one to the other, and then she put a hand to her forehead as though there were cobwebs there. Old people, she told herself sadly, were so busy inventing problems where no problems really existed.

"Did you think I'd get mad at Tommy and raise a fuss because there was another girl with him when his car smashed up?" she asked, and her tone was one suitable for the explanation of a ridiculously simple problem to a rather stupid child. "Don't you realize even yet that I know Tommy, and that he couldn't be unfaithful to me if he tried? Why, we're like two halves of the same person! Whatever happened, I'd always know that Tommy wasn't to blame, because he loves me as much as I love him. And you can't love somebody unless you trust him the way I trust Tommy—the way he trusts me."

She looked from one to the other, and then she said with a trace of her usual good manners, "And now, if you'll excuse me, I have to get back to Tommy. He might wake up and call for me, and I've got to be there when he does."

She walked away down the corridor, a slender, pretty girl, her head held high.

15

NORA LOOKED up from her desk just before closing time, as Mary Jordan appeared in the doorway, smiling, a large brown envelope in her hands.

"Oh, come on in, Mary," Nora urged hospitably, rising to greet her.

Mary laughed and laid the envelope on Nora's desk.

"It's all there, the price of Connie's dress," she announced proudly. "I honestly think we could have raised twice as much, because everybody who knows Connie wanted to contribute. But there *is* a problem."

"Oh?"

"It's about the wedding, Nora."

"Now, don't tell me it's off."

"Goodness, no!" Mary scoffed swiftly. "We wouldn't *allow* that! No, the problem is that everybody who contributed wants to attend the wedding, and I'm afraid you wouldn't have room for all of us. So if it's all right with you, we thought it would be nice to have the wedding in the church, and then maybe a reception at your place later? Would that be all right?"

"Of course it would! That would be wonderful!" Nora answered eagerly. "I'll lure Connie and Hank out to my place for dinner, and then we'll bundle her into her 'custom-made gown' and whiz her right out to the church! That will be just perfect!"

"Well, the church seats more than six hundred, and there can be standees." Mary laughed as Nora's brows went up a little. "I told you Connie and Hank had a lot of friends!"

"They are lucky!"

"I think so, too," Mary admitted frankly, and stood up. "I'll have to run now. You've been swell about all this, Nora, and we are all very grateful."

"Pish-tosh!" Nora protested gaily. "I've been up to my neck in wedding plans ever since I came here, but this is the one wedding that I'm personally concerned with making the most beautiful of all."

Mary thanked her and hurried off just as the closing bell rang out through the store. And Nora picked up the envelope and hurried with it to Mrs. Anstruthers, who was just closing her desk.

"It's payment," Nora explained, as she put down the envelope, "for Connie Terrell's frock."

Mrs. Anstruthers' delicately penciled brows drew together as she opened the envelope, looked curiously at its contents, and then up at Nora.

"Connie Terrell?" she repeated, puzzled. "And in cash?"

Nora nodded. "She's the girl in the basement store who wanted more than anything in the world to be truly beautiful when she walked down the church aisle to marry her beloved. And it's in cash because there was a—well, a sort of financial crisis in Connie's life, and she had to cancel her plans. But her friends and co-workers were determined she should have her wedding after all—so they contributed. It's all there, including the sales tax."

Mrs. Anstruthers nodded slowly, as once more she examined the contents of the envelope: a thick sheaf of bills, most of them ones and fives. Then she looked up at Nora.

"Has the dress been completed, delivered?" she asked.

"It's being delivered to my house tomorrow," Nora answered.

Mrs. Anstruthers listened while Nora explained, and then she smiled, slid the envelope into her desk drawer and locked it.

"So this is one wedding in which you became personally involved?" she commented, and her smile was surprisingly warm. "Makes it a lot more fun, doesn't it?"

"Oh, yes!" Nora agreed.

"Well, I'll turn this payment in to the proper office in the morning," said Mrs. Anstruthers. As Nora turned to go, she added quietly, "How do you feel about your mother marrying again, Nora?"

Startled, Nora turned swiftly.

"Oh, I'm very happy for her, Mrs. Anstruthers, because *she* seems happy about it," she answered with simple honesty.

"Good girl!" Mrs. Anstruthers smiled at her and added, "Good night."

Nora came out into the hot, late afternoon and found Jay waiting for her. There was a small and happy glow in her heart as he came wading through the crowd toward her and guided her down the street toward the parking lot.

"So the Larrimore-Neilson nuptials went off without a hitch," he began as he slid beneath the wheel and grinned down at her.

"Oh, did they?" Nora asked, and laughed. "Well, after all, why not? Belloti's was in charge."

He managed the car out of the parking lot, watching narrowly for a chance to slip the car into north-bound traffic and slid to a stop at the nearest traffic light before he spoke again.

"Oh, Connie and Hank are going to be married at the church," she began eagerly.

"But what about your plans? Haven't you already arranged for flowers, decoration?"

"Oh, but when Mary Jordan brought the money to pay for her dress, she said everybody who had contributed wanted to attend the wedding and mentioned that Connie had always wanted a church wedding and anyway, my place wasn't big enough. The church seats six hundred, and Mary added there would, of course, be standees!"

"My sainted aunt!" Jay murmured, as the car slipped

ahead. "I can't imagine knowing a dozen friends I'd want to see me step off the deep end."

"I can't either," Nora admitted, and felt a slight lessening of her high spirits. "They are two very lucky people, aren't they?"

"Very," he answered. And after a moment, "Too bad about the Livingston girl and her boy friend."

Nora asked sharply, "What's happened?"

Jay stared at her puzzled. "Well, you read about it yourself. The guy smashed his car up with another gal in it. You don't think the Livingston gal will marry him now, do you?"

Nora laughed. "Well, for your information, my friend, Penny had the last fitting on her gown yesterday. And she and Tommy are going to be married in the hospital just as soon as his doctor says they may!"

"You mean she forgave him for being with another gal when the car crashed?" he asked, puzzled.

Nora studied him for a long moment and then said quietly, "You don't know much about women, do you, Jay?"

"No, ma'am." Jay's tone was crisp.

"Well, Penny's and Tommy's case is very simple and very easy to understand," Nora told him. "They love each other; and when you love somebody you have faith in him. That's what Penny has: love for Tommy and, therefore, complete and unquestioning faith in him. See how simple it is?"

Jay drove for a few blocks in complete silence, attending to the sluggishly flowing river of traffic that surrounded him, before the cut-off to the expressway thinned it out a bit.

"Simple?" he repeated then, relaxing ever so slightly. "Well, yes, I suppose it is. I would have thought she'd have thrown him over with a dull thud."

"Just as you thought Allene would throw Brock over because he was guilty of the sin of dining with me while she was out of town?" Nora reminded him gently, though her eyes were bright and accusing.

"Oho! We're back to that, are we?" Jay asked ruefully.

"Well, you must admit that you were pretty intolerant and very insulting and generally unpleasant about what was the most innocent and accidental meeting!" she pointed out. "As accidental as the night you and I happened to see them at the Biltmore."

"Accidental? When he had left word around town to be notified if you happened to wander in alone?"

Nora sat up straight and her eyes flashed.

"I wouldn't mind all this idiotic business if I'd been pursuing Brock. But under the circumstances, it's just a little too much!" she told him warmly.

"I don't think I'd mind so much," Jay said thoughtfully after a moment, "if you hadn't come down off your pedestal."

Nora blinked in amazement.

"What pedestal?" she demanded.

"The one I put you on the first time I met you," he admitted frankly. "You see, I was sort of planning to fall in love with you."

"Don't be an idiot! You don't plan to fall in love any more than you plan to be struck by lightning! It just happens!"

He seemed honestly surprised.

"It does?" he asked after a moment.

"It does indeed, my friend, as you're going to find out one of these days, and I surely hope I'll be there to see it when it does!"

Jay turned the car neatly through the entrance to the drive up to the old stone house. He brought it to a halt and nodded.

"Know something?" He was still thoughtful. "I've got a hunch—a very strong hunch—you will be."

For no reason at all, Nora found her color mounting and, to disguise it, scrambled out of the car and went marching up the steps and into the house, leaving him to follow or not as he chose.

She reached her room and closed the door behind her and stood for a long moment, leaning her back against the closed panels. After a little, she heard Jay come up the stairs, and then his own door closed behind him across the hall.

She still stood there. And then she tensed as she heard a brisk rap on the door across the hall, and Lucy's voice, gay, lilting, calling Jay.

"Hi, hurry it up, will you?" she called. "We're starving, and the longer you make us wait, the more it's going to cost you, pal!"

Nora's breath seemed to hang suspended as she waited for Jay's answer. And then she heard his door open and close, heard the low murmur of his voice answering Lucy, and caught the gay laughter with which Lucy answered him. Finally their voices faded as they went down the stairs and the outer door closed hard behind them.

It was not until then that Nora moved stiffly from her position against her closed door, went awkwardly across the room and dropped into a chair.

16

Connie was touchingly pleased at the dinner invitation, when Nora found her in the cafeteria and extended the bid.

"It's awfully good of you, Nora," she said humbly, her thin young face touched with a shy smile that did not reach to her eyes, "especially after I had to give up my dress. Was Mrs. Anstruthers very angry?"

Nora had to bite her tongue to keep back the announcement that the dress was still hers. Instead, she smiled and said, "Oh, no, not a bit. Matter of fact, she had a client it will just fit, with only the smallest alterations."

She set her teeth hard at the bleak look that swept

Connie's face before she managed to say valiantly, "Oh, that's good. I'm awfully glad."

It was all that Nora could do to keep the secret. And yet she and Mary Jordan had discussed the fact that if Connie knew about their plans, her fierce, hot pride would make her refuse to accept the dress or go through with the wedding. And that, of course, must not happen.

"How is your father, Connie?" she asked gently.

"Oh, the doctors say he's going to be all right, and that the operation will make him almost as good as new." Connie smiled faintly. "He's distressed because Hank and I can't have the wedding we'd planned. I've managed to convince him that I don't mind a bit. He doesn't want us to postpone the wedding, because he says it's bad luck. So Hank and I will just go around to the parsonage and be married."

She looked up at Nora, and a small, valiant smile was carefully in place on her strained young face.

"And being married to Hank is really all that matters, I know," she said earnestly, as much to convince herself as Nora. "It was pretty silly of me to want a big, fancy, splashy wedding. People in our circumstances would be just plain foolish." She caught her breath, blinked hard against the threatening tears and rose. "I'll have to rush, Nora, thank you for asking us to dinner. It will make up for a lot."

Nora sat and watched her as she hurried out of the cafeteria, and wished that she need not go through the next two days believing that her cherished plans were to be smashed.

"Being married to Hank is really all that matters," she had said.

Nora sighed and got up. There were other clients waiting for her services, because as soon as Penny Livingston and Allene Larrimore had passed from her hands into marriage, she had been assigned three others.

The newspapers had made much of the wedding of young Penelope Livingston, the season's loveliest and most popular deb, and Thomas Elton Parker IV. The marriage had taken place in the hospital, said the news-papers, where Mr. Parker was recovering from a nearly fatal auto accident. The hospital room had been banked with flowers that completely concealed the walls. The bridegroom had been lavishly bandaged and the bride had entered the room, exquisite, said the papers, in an embroidered lace and tulle frock, carrying a shower of white orchids.

Nora had smiled as she had read the account and had been able to visualize the whole scene. It was like Penny, she told herself with a warm feeling for the girl, that she would be married in her Belloti gown even if the wedding had to take place in a hospital room instead of a church. Remembering the way she had looked at the final fitting of her gown, and when she had posed for her wedding photographs in Belloti's studio, Nora knew that Tommy must have looked at her in awed wonder at her beauty. Nora sighed and went back to work.

Jay stood with her at the entrance to the big double parlor, fragrant with the scent of flowers, and whistled softly.

"You really went all out, didn't you?" he marveled.

"It was way past time there should have been a wedding here," she told him, and felt her color rise beneath his startled gaze. "A wedding reception, anyway!"

"And you're doing all this for a girl you barely know!" Jay said quietly.

"I'm having fun," she assured him firmly, "helping to make a dream come true for a girl like Connie. She's—well, she's such a nice girl! And Hank's one of the best."

"Fairy godmother to Cinderella, eh?" Jay mocked her gently.

Nora's head went up.

"And what's wrong with that?" she demanded hotly.

"Nothing! Nothing at all! I think you're swell!" Jay assured her hastily. "So put down that gun, gal—I ain't even about to throw cold water."

Nora turned, startled, at the sound of the door chimes,

and swiftly drew the door of the long, double parlor closed.

"They're here," she told Jay swiftly. "Now you know what to do. Hank's your responsibility."

"Yessum," said Jay meekly, as Emma, smiling broadly, opened the door and Connie and Hank stepped hesitantly into the big, handsome reception hall.

Nora and Jay greeted them warmly, and Nora said briskly to Connie, "Come on upstairs with me, Connie. Jay will look after Hank. You and I have time for a little chat before dinner."

"This is a beautiful house," said Connie soberly, as she followed Nora up the wide stairs and through the door into Nora's room.

She stood just inside the room, and the first thing her eyes fell on was the dress spread with the utmost care across Nora's bed. It was a dress that Connie knew as she knew the inside of her own heart; a gown that looked as though it had been woven of moonbeams, so delicately airy was it, its color of palest blue visible only where there were folds.

"My dress," she said at last, her tone a mere breath of sound. And then, after a stunned moment of incredulous wonder, she looked at Nora. "My dress, Nora?"

"Well, I'd like to know who else's?" Nora was blinking back tears at Connie's tone and expression. "Come on, let's get you into it."

Connie drew back, and now she was so pale that there was a hint of blue at her temples.

"But Nora, I told you I can't afford it," she protested.

"Connie darling, it's your wedding present, from your friends and co-workers at the store," Nora told her gently.

Color poured into Connie's face and her head went up.

"Oh, but I couldn't let them do that," she said wildly.

"You can't stop them," Nora told her, and added gently, "Connie, you are the luckiest girl in the world to have friends like those people who work with you. They love you, Connie, and they wanted to do this for you to show you their affection. You aren't going to be too stiff-necked and too arrogantly proud to deny them the expression of that affection, are you? You couldn't be that petty-minded."

"But the people I work with, Nora, all their heavy expenses—families. They can't afford anything like this," Connie protested shakily. "It took me almost six years to save enough money. I can't let them—I *can't*."

"Connie, there were so many of them. The contributions were no more than five dollars from any group; most of the contributions were a dollar each. Some of the maids in the fitting and alteration rooms and in the basement grill room contributed. Don't you see, Connie? It was something they all wanted very much to do, and they did it, and they are very proud and happy about it. But if you're going to be mean-minded and deny them that happiness—"

"But—oh, Nora, I knew I should never have wanted a dress that cost such a lot, and I thought my not being able to have it was punishment for being so extravagant," Connie wailed, and tears slid down her face.

There was a knock at the door, and it opened to reveal Lucy and Susan, lovely in airy formal frocks, saying happily, "Ready for us?"

"Connie, these are friends of mine who are going to be your bridesmaids," Nora introduced them. "She isn't sure, girls, that she's going to accept the dress, after all."

"What?" gasped Lucy, outraged at the idea. "Why, Connie, you should be spanked! It's a lovesome frock! And if it would fit me, I'd take it away from you! Here, let's get you dressed. We can't keep all the wedding guests waiting, you know. And Jay says it's a long drive to the church."

Connie gasped and allowed herself to be pushed down on the stool in front of Nora's dressing table as she looked from one to the other of the laughing faces grouped about her.

"The church?" she gasped.

Nora said gently, "Look, honey, I know we've bowled you over with all this. But we knew if it wasn't a surprise, you'd probably dig in your heels and be a stubborn little mule. The wedding guests are already assembling, I have no doubt, at the church; so how's about climbing into your 'glad rags' and getting started?"

"Oh, Nora," gasped Connie helplessly. "Does Hank know?"

"Well, of course he does. Mary Jordan took care of Hank, and Jay's briefing him right now." Nora grinned as she helped Connie out of her limp cotton dress and, with Lucy's and Susan's aid, lifted the exquisite mass of lace and tulle and satin over Connie's bowed head.

Connie straightened as she faced the mirror and the folds of the gown fell into place about her slender body. The veil which Nora carefully adjusted was a cap of palest blue satin, outlined in seed pearls, with a floating shoulder-length web of tulle.

Lucy stood back when they had finished and looked Connie over from the top of her head to the tip of her feet, in slippers of satin exactly the shade of the dress, and stockings so cobweb thin that they were all but invisible.

"Now," said Lucy softly, "if only I can find me a man, Nora, you'll have yourself another client. Talk about miracle-workers! Connie, you're—you're—" words failed her.

"It's the dress," Connie explained earnestly and touched the delicate stuff with gentle fingers, her eyes wide and awed as she studied herself in the mirror. "I could never look like this if it wasn't for the dress."

"Well, we'll see what your boy friend says when he sees you," Lucy promised, and walked slowly around Connie, studying her critically. "Every hair in place; every thread out of sight; stocking seams straight as a die. You'll do, Connie, you'll do."

Nora opened the door, and the four of them filed out to the top of the landing. Connie stopped there and looked down the beautifully curving stairs to where Hank and

Jay stood waiting. And Nora, behind her, saw the look of startled wonder that lit Hank's face as Connie went slowly down the stairs, walking with the unconscious arrogance of a woman who knows that once in her life she looks her very loveliest.

Hank watched her as she came down the stairs, and Nora saw that Jay was watching Hank with a curious alertness.

To Hank and Connie it was as though they were alone in the world.

Connie paused on the bottom step, and Hank's face lifted, his eyes bright with wonder.

"Connie?" he asked uncertainly, and then he smiled. "But of course. You're lovely, honey; but then you always were."

Jay looked up at the three girls who were coming slowly down the stairs, and his eyebrows raised slightly. And Nora was reminded of the time when he had said that no amount of fancy dressing was necessary to make a man realize the girl he loved was beautiful. She knew that Jay, too, was remembering that; knew it as, somehow, she felt she would always know at least something of what Jay was thinking.

Jay broke the taut silence by nudging Hank and saying in a conspiratorial whisper, "Aren't you forgetting something, son?"

Hank seemed to come out of the daze in which the sight of Connie had thrown him, and straightened, glanced bewilderedly at Jay and then at the box Jay was holding out to him.

"Oh—oh, yes, thanks," said Hank, took the cover from the box and held out to Connie a small white prayer book topped with a single Cattleya orchid.

Connie's eyes widened and her white-gloved hands shook slightly as she looked down at the orchid.

"An orchid!" she breathed. "I never had an orchid before."

"Well, no," Hank said with an earnestness that was very touching to those who heard him. "And I'm afraid you may not have another one soon, honey. But for to-night it had to be an orchid. I'll try very hard to manage one every year."

"You needn't, Hank. Just love me. Who wants orchids?" Connie told him tremulously, and there was a threat of tears in her voice.

"Hi," warned Lucy firmly, "no tears to spoil that make-up—I won't have it! You look simply scrumptious! And this is no time for tears. Let's get going!"

Jay turned to Nora, his eyes sweeping over her summer frock of white with its splashy pale green leaf-print, and the green-like hat.

"Ready?" he asked, and Nora laughed.

"Oh, I'm not in the wedding party," she told him gaily. "And this is supposed to be quite suitable for a June wedding, if you're only a guest."

"Or a fairy godmother?" suggested Jay softly, as they all moved towards the door. "It's quite suitable for a bride, it seems to me; only I am only an ignorant male and I wouldn't know."

Outside, Jay's car held Nora, Lucy and Susan. A taxi waited for Hank and Connie, and the two cars set off across town toward the church where the guests were assembling.

Nora slipped into a pew, and Lucy and Susan arranged themselves to lead the way down the aisle at the proper moment. Connie stood breathless for a moment, and then a tall young boy, probably seventeen or so, came toward her, grinning bashfully.

"Hi, Sis. Boy, do you ever look swell," he greeted her. "Mom said I was to hand you over to Hank when the parson says the right words, since Pop can't be here. Want to trust me not to fall over my big feet going down the aisle, and to be sure not to lose my voice at the last moment?"

"Oh, Teddy!" Connie caught her breath as she slid her hand through her brother's arm. Behind her Lucy warned her sternly, "Shed one tear to ruin your make-up and I'll clout you, so help me!"

Hank and Jay had vanished. Now, as the girls waited in the vestibule, they appeared at the altar beside the minister, looking so far away that Teddy had to swallow before he could get his nerve up to take what looked to him like the longest walk he had ever taken.

The sound of the organ playing softly reached them, and the strains of "Here Comes the Bride!" Lucy winked at Susan, straightened above the bouquet of snapdragon and delphinium Jay had provided for each of the bridesmaids and walked forward. Susan followed a few paces behind, and then Teddy and Connie.

There was a small stir and rustling through the church as they came into view, heads turned, and there was a murmur, "Isn't she lovely?"

Connie and Teddy reached the group in front of the altar, and the gentle, white-haired old minister opened his Book at the Marriage Service.

"Dearly beloved, we are gathered together—"

Listening to the solemn, beautiful words, Nora spent a moment wondering about all the many, many times those words had been read above girls wearing Belloti gowns; girls wearing cotton frocks; wearing a radiance of happiness that outshone anything that they might be wearing. None of them, she was quite sure, had ever looked lovelier or more radiant than Connie, as Hank bent his head and kissed her at the minister's final words. He offered her his arm and with a smile of such beaming delight that Nora felt a mist of tears in her eyes as they turned and came back up the aisle.

17

IT WAS WELL after midnight before the last guest had gone. Lucy and Susan had gone upstairs, chattering happily with Mr. and Mrs. Blake, and now Nora and Jay were alone in the big double parlor where the reception had taken place.

Nora sat limply in a big chair, her head back, her eyes closed.

Jay prowled the room, eyeing her now and then, taking in the havoc in the wake of the party: the tall baskets of flowers, the potted palms and plants, the table with its plate of limp sandwiches, overflowing ashtrays, the delicate pink rosebuds and the blue delphinium looking less than crisp.

"Shame to waste all this," Jay offered after a moment. "Ought to be something we could do about using it all again. Like, say, another wedding."

Nora smiled faintly.

"For that you have to have a bride and a groom," she reminded him drowsily, "also three days' waiting period for a marriage license. By that time there'd be nothing left here but the palms, and the florist's men will pick them up in the morning."

Jay nodded, and she asked curiously, "Did you have someone in mind? Someone in particular, I mean?"

Jay scowled at her thoughtfully.

"Well, yes, as a matter of fact I did," he admitted.

For a moment she met his eyes, and then her own closed and she lay back once more, limp and tired. She had suspected this from the first time she had seen him with Lucy. And Lucy was waiting eagerly for him to ask her.

Emma, hovering in the doorway, said anxiously, "Miss Nora, you look plumb beat. You go on upstairs and get to bed. I'll clean up all this."

Nora opened one eye and regarded her with a sleepy smile.

"Correction, Emma! We'll both go on to bed, and then we'll both clean up this mess tomorrow. It won't take long with both of us working—and tomorrow is my day off, praises be!"

"With three of us working," Jay pointed out, "it'll take even less time."

"You're going to help?" Nora mocked him lightly. "It isn't your day off and you know it."

"I made special arrangements, madam!" he assured her loftily. "I took it for granted that the aftermath of all this fuss and feathers would need a man's strong right arm."

The doorbell chimed and Nora sat up, looking puzzled.

"Now who in the world—it's after two o'clock!" she gasped, as Emma went to answer the door's summons. And then Nora stiffened and came to her feet at the light musical voice speaking to Emma. "It's Mother!"

She ran out into the hall, where Celia stood, a distinguished-looking man in his early sixties just behind her, his eyes taking in the scene with an amused but lively appreciation.

"Mother!" Nora gasped as she hugged Celia. "I thought you were in Europe."

Celia kissed the air an inch from Nora's cheek, ever mindful of her exquisite make-up, and removed herself from Nora's too ardent embrace.

"Oh, Gordy had unexpected business in San Juan, so we flew there and he attended to it. And then when we started back—we'd already lost our reservations on the *Raffaello,* of course—Gordy made new reservations. So he included one for you, and we stopped by to pick you up and take you with us." Celia spoke carelessly, as though there could not possibly be any objection to her plans, as she walked across the hall and to the parlor doorway.

She stopped there and gasped, her eyes wide, swinging from one part of the room to the other before she turned accusingly on Nora.

"What in heaven's name has been going on here?" she demanded sharply.

Nora laughed. "A wedding reception, Mother. We haven't had time to put things straight."

The distinguished-looking man was apparently quite content just to be a spectator, though his eyes on Nora were warm and friendly.

Celia gave a small, shocked scream and whirled about to look at Jay, who met her eyes, a small grin on his mouth, his hands jammed deeply into his pockets.

"A wedding reception!" Celia gasped. "Nora! You haven't—you didn't—oh, Nora, you—"

Nora laughed. "No, Mother, I haven't! I didn't! I'm still a spinster, and the reception was for a Belloti bride, a friend of mine."

Celia's eyes widened slightly.

"Oh, how nice! Anyone I know?" she asked with interest.

Nora shook her head. "I'm afraid not, Mother. She works in the baesment store at Belloti's."

Celia's outrage was frank and not pretty.

"A shopgirl being entertained here?"

Gordon MacFarlaine's face stiffened a trifle and his eyes on his lovely wife were faintly chill.

"Aren't you forgetting, Mother? I'm a shopgirl now."

Celia made a little gesture of dismissal.

"Oh, that's nonsense!" she sniffed daintily. "You're giving that ridiculous job up immediately. We'll put the house on the market, in a good realtor's hands, and then you're going abroad with Gordy and me."

Nora looked at the man who was watching her with a curiously intent look and suddenly realized she hadn't even spoken to him. She smiled and came to him and held out her hand.

"How do you do?" she said pleasantly. "By now you've gathered that I'm Nora, and I know, of course, who you are. But what do I call you?"

"Could you manage Gordon?"

"May I?"

"I hope you will."

She turned to Jay.

"And, Mr. MacFarlaine, this is my friend, Jay Murphy," Nora said, smiling at Jay. "My mother's husband, Jay."

The men shook hands, exchanging polite greetings, and Celia cut in briskly, "When Gordy and I were driving by on our way to the Biltmore, we saw all the lights and I was upset so we stopped to see if anything was wrong. Now that we know, we'll be running along. We'll pick you up tomorrow after dinner, Nora. Don't bother packing very much. We'll have grand fun shopping in New York, and then later in Paris."

"I'm not going, Mother," Nora said firmly.

Celia stared at her, annoyed.

"Oh, for heaven's sake, Nora, don't be difficult! Of course you're going—isn't she, Gordy?" she appealed tardily to him.

Gordon MacFarlaine smiled at Nora, a friendly, warm smile.

"We'd be very happy to have you, Nora, if you'd like to join us," he told her with such utter sincerity that Nora felt a real liking for him.

"Thank you, Gordon. That's lovely of you, and I'm really very grateful," she said quietly, and shook her head. "But I like my job and I'm doing well with it, so I want to keep on. Besides, the house is filled with tenants who are my friends, and I wouldn't want them turned out in the street."

"Nora, you're still as stubborn, as selfish as ever," Celia cried out hotly. "You never think of anyone but yourself."

"Hi, now, wait a doggone minute." Jay spoke for the first time, his voice curt and angry. "You can't say that about Nora. She's the most unselfish gal that ever lived —always thinking of other people."

Celia turned on him haughtily.

"Young man, I'd thank you to mind your own business," she said icily. "Nora is my daughter, and she's closing this house, putting it on the market and going with Gordy and me to Europe!"

Jay met her furious eyes and then looked at Nora.

"Are you?" he asked quietly.

"Of course not!" Nora answered.

Celia drew herself up, but before she could speak, Gordon said quietly, but in a tone that made them all turn and look at him, "What do you say we all sleep on the proposition and discuss it tomorrow? We're all tired now, and nervous and a bit irritable. So let's wait until tomorrow to decide, shall we?"

Celia cried out, "But there's nothing to discuss, Gordy. She's my daughter and I say she's coming with us. And that settles it."

"I'm afraid it doesn't, Mother. I'm over twenty-one and quite capable of making my own decisions," Nora reminded her.

For a moment Celia's eyes locked with Nora's, and neither of them showed the slightest inclination to yield to the other. Gordon glanced at Jay, exchanged an amused man-to-man glance at the foibles of womenkind and drew Celia toward the door.

"We'll see you tomorrow, my dear," he said, and nodded to Jay.

"You needn't go to a hotel, Mother," Nora said placatingly. "Your rooms are just as you left them."

Over her shoulder Celia said curtly, "We prefer a hotel to a rooming house."

"Don't mind her, Nora; she's upset," said Gordon. Nora laughed, at which he raised his eyebrows, looking a bit startled.

"Oh, I understand Mother thoroughly, Gordon," Nora told him.

"I wish I did," Gordon admitted frankly.

Celia said crossly, "I wish you'd stop discussing me as though I were somewhere else. Come along, Gordy. I'm tired and bored!"

Gordon said good night, and the door closed behind them. Jay and Nora stood in silence for a moment. Emma looked from one to the other, then slipped off down the hall to her own quarters.

The silence between Nora and Jay stretched until at

last tension developed and Nora said with unconvincing briskness, "Well, I think I'll trot off to bed. It's been quite a day!"

"It has that," Jay agreed. "And you have a lot of thinking to do, too. Be sure you make up your mind the right way, Nora."

Nora's eyes widened a little.

"The right way, Jay? What *is* the right way?"

"That's something you alone can decide, Nora," Jay told her slowly. "But your mother's suggestion makes sense. Sell the place here, bank yourself a small fortune, and then hit the high spots abroad with her and the Mac-Farlaine guy. You wouldn't have to hand him your bills if you didn't want to, though he'd probably want to make you a handsome allowance."

"Jay, you're being silly!" Nora protested warmly. "I don't want to go to Europe or to sell the house." She broke off, and her eyes widened beneath the impact of a sudden thought. "Why, Jay, I *don't* want to sell the house!"

It was a surprising thought, and for a moment she turned it about in her mind. Then she looked up at him, childishly puzzled.

"Isn't that funny?" she demanded. "I've been wanting to sell the place ever since Dad died, and I couldn't without Mother's consent. And now that I have her consent, I no longer want to sell. Isn't that crazy?"

Jay's eyes were amused, yet there was tenderness in them.

"Well, no, I don't suppose so," he answered. "With the place rented as it is, it's meeting its own expenses and a bit over. And there's no danger of its value dropping; the longer you hold onto it, the more valuable it will be."

Nora drew a deep breath and smiled at him.

"Well, thanks for making me see that," she told him.

His smile was tight, mirthless.

"Always glad to be of service," he answered, and stood for a long moment eyeing her with a look she had never seen in his eyes before. "I have a strong feeling that there are a lot of things I should make you see, Nora, if I can only do it without my own plans getting in the way."

Before she could question him, his mirthless smile was gone and he was looking at her doggedly, grimly even.

"I take that back," he said quickly. "I have no plans, only hopes. And they're getting dimmer by the minute."

He stood up, thrust his hands deep into his pockets, strode the length of the room and paused at the table where bowls of flowers flanked the tall silver epergne.

Jay turned and studied her for a long moment before he came back to her and dropped into a deep chair across from her. He leaned forward, his arms resting on his knees, his hands loosely locked between them, and his eyes on her with an intensity that somehow made her heart leap and then plunge into a wild, tumultuous beating.

"What your mother and your stepfather offer you, Nora, is something any girl in her right mind would regard as a dream come true." He spoke very slowly, as though he dredged the words up from deep in his consciousness. "Wait a minute; let me finish. Think of it, and think hard, Nora. They are offering you a new life quite different from anything you've ever known. So how can you be so sure you wouldn't like it? Paris, Rome, all the finest shops, where instead of helping other girls choose fabulous clothes, you'd be choosing them for yourself, and wearing them to all sorts of exciting, glamorous parties. You'd be meeting exciting people; people whose names are household words, if I may coin a phrase. You have to think of all that, Nora, and think hard about it, before you decide."

Nora was silent for a moment, and then she met his eyes.

"Most of that I've already known, Jay," she told him quietly. "I've been to Paris, Rome and London during my last year at finishing school. For two years before my father died, I thought we were so rich that—well, that there was nothing I couldn't have if I really wanted it. And my debutante year just made me more certain that I was, if I may coin a phrase, Fortune's darling. There were the fabulous clothes, the parties, the dancing until dawn and sleeping until tea time, and then another round of parties and more dancing until dawn. And you know something, Jay? I grew bored!"

Jay said swiftly, "Oh, come now."

"It's quite true, Jay! It stopped being any fun, and I stopped wanting to ride the merry-go-round. And then Dad died, and there wasn't much money, and I could see how spoiled and selfish and extravagant and heedless I'd been. I sort of woke up. And I've never ceased to mourn that I didn't wake up while Dad was still here so I could stop driving him into bankruptcy. That's what we did, Mother and I. The poor sweet tried to keep up with our demands, and then there was a heart attack. He died in his office, Jay, trying to scrape up money to keep us going our crazy, cock-eyed pace. I'll never quite get over that, Jay."

Jay watched her for a moment, and then he said gently, "Well, honey, I imagine he understood. He wanted only the best for you—he must have been very proud of you."

"How could he have been?" Nora asked huskily. "I didn't do anything to make him proud of me. I just spent money as though it might be going out of style, and raced around like a silly ballerina on a music box."

He was wordless before the pain in her eyes and in her voice, and at last she went on in that husky, tear-threatened voice, "So now I've got a job; the days have point to them. There's something to get up for in the morning; there are things at the shop I'm responsible for. Oh, I know it's not important, my job. Not really important like—oh, like being a trained nurse and taking care of sick and ailing people; or doing social work, helping people in the slums. I had a taste of that while I was doing my probationary training so I could join the Junior League. So I know that what I'm doing isn't really important. But it's my job, Jay, and I love it. I love having a job, and I don't want to give it up to go back to just dancing all night and sleeping all day and the whole crazy merry-go-round. And that's what it would be with Mother and Gordon."

"You might find the most important job in the world if you went with them, Nora."

Her eyes widened and then narrowed in surprise.

"What does that mean?" she asked in honest curiosity.

"Marriage," said Jay levelly.

"Oh," said Nora, and her voice sounded a trifle flat. "Oh, yes, I suppose I might. Mother would do her utmost to find me a 'suitable prospect,' I know."

"That she would," Jay growled, "whether you considered him suitable or not."

There was a moment of silence between them, and then Jay asked flatly, "You're not—well, shall we say emotionally involved with anyone here, Nora?"

Color burned high in her cheeks, but she met his eyes levelly.

"I'm afraid I am, Jay," she answered quietly.

He stiffened, and his jaw hardened as though she had struck him hard.

"Oh?" he said at last, and his tone was harsh. "I didn't know."

"That's because you didn't want to know, Jay."

For a moment he could only stare at her, puzzled and uneasy.

"I'm afraid I don't get that," he said at last.

"Don't be frightened, Jay." She had her voice under control now and could smile faintly at him. "I know how terrified you are of marriage."

"I resent that!" Jay snapped sharply. "I'm not afraid of marriage. I just don't want it to be to the, well—the wrong girl."

"Nobody does, of course," Nora told him. "But it's hard to know sometimes just who is right and who is wrong."

"Well, I'll know," Jay said grimly. "And when I do—" He broke off and studied her for a moment, and she continued to meet his eyes steadily.

At last she said very low, "Yes, Jay?"

"I knew, twenty-four hours after I met you, that you were the right girl for me," he said with a sort of restrained violence.

Wide-eyed, her breath held suspended, Nora stared at him.

"And don't look at me like that," Jay said harshly. "You must have known that as well as I did."

"I didn't, Jay—truly I didn't," she stammered.

"Oh, no?" His tone gave it the lie. "Then where's that famous woman's intuition that we hear so much about? Why do you suppose I suggested tonight, just before your mother barged in here, that you and I stage our own wedding here so we wouldn't waste all this decoration?"

Nora said wildly, "You didn't suggest we stage *our own* wedding, Jay! You just said it was a shame to waste all this. I didn't dream you wanted me to marry you. *Do* you, Jay?"

"Well, what in blazes do you think I want?"

"You've been awfully busy trying to persuade me to go away with Mother and Gordon. How could I know you didn't really want me to go?" she sputtered, childishly indignant.

"I didn't feel I had the right to try to persuade you to do anything so silly as staying here and marrying me."

"You wouldn't have had to persuade me, Jay," she told him with beautiful, unashamed simplicity. "All you had to do was say, 'Nora, I love you and I want you to stay.'"

A look of awe and wonder touched his face, and he stood up and looked down at her, his hands jammed into his pockets as though he were afraid to trust them not to reach out to her in this moment of shimmering joy that seemed to him too perfect to be real.

"Will you, Nora?" he asked at last, his voice no more than a thread of sound.

Nora looked up at him from the depths of the big chair, and now there was a lovely color in her face and her eyes were shining.

"Will I *what*, Jay?" she asked softly.

"Marry me, of course. What else have I been talking about?"

"I'm not quite sure," she admitted, and now there was a tremulous smile touching her soft mouth. "Mostly you've been trying to persuade me to go away, sell the house, give up my job—"

"Stop clowning, Nora." His tone was so sharp that she gave a tiny start. "Will you marry me?"

"Why, Jay?"

His brows drew together in an angry scowl.

"Why? Why, because I love you, of course, you little dope!"

Nora lifted one hand in a little airy gesture, her eyes brimming with loving laughter.

"Well, why didn't you *say* so?"

His brows black with anger, Jay barked, "Do I *have* to say it?"

Nora nodded with an air of solemnity, despite the twinkle dancing in her starry eyes.

"Well, I understand it's expected." Her voice was low and very sweet, but ever so faintly touched with mockery.

"You are," Jay stated flatly, hands bunched into fists and still jammed into his pockets, his head a little on one side, his brows furrowed, "the most exasperating female it's ever been my fortune to meet."

"Exasperating?" she repeated as though not quite sure she understood him.

"Exasperating! Like—oh, like trying to capture a moonbeam—or a butterfly that waits until you are ready to close your hand over it and then slips away in flight!" he insisted. "What would you like me to do? Drop down on one knee, a hand on my heart, and declaim, 'Miss Robinson—Miss Nora—*may* I call you Nora?—will you do me the very great honor of becoming my wife?"

Nora said sedately, "Well, that would be nice, but you really needn't go to all that bother. It will be perfectly all right if you'll just say tenderly, 'Nora, my dear, I love you.' "

Jay bent down suddenly, his hands gripping her shoulders as he pulled her up and into his arms.

"Nora, my blessed darling, I adore you," he said huskily, his lips against her ear. "Will you please put me out of my misery and marry me?"

Nora clung to him, her cheek against his, feeling against her outspread hands on his chest the hard, exultant beating of his heart.

"Why, yes, darling, thanks a lot, I'd love to," she told him joyously, and lifted her face for his kiss.

There was an interval of radiance so perfect that any faintest word would have profaned it; and then Jay drew a deep, hard breath and held her a few inches away from him so that he could look down into her flushed face, her shining eyes.

"You may be making a big mistake," he warned her, his voice not quite steady. "I'll work my fingers off to take care of you, but I can't promise you custom-made gowns and orchids and strings of pearls. I will guarantee you a diamond ring—even a microscope so you can really see it, because it may be pretty small."

Nora laughed richly, framed his face between her two hands and set her mouth on his as she murmured softly, "Oh, shut up and kiss me again!"

And Jay, escaping from the unaccustomed sentimentality of the moment, managed to say huskily, "Always happy to oblige!"

THE END

Belmont Romance Books

USE SPECIAL ORDER FORM ON LAST PAGE TO PURCHASE THESE NEW BELMONT BOOKS

- [ ] **LOVE IS ENOUGH,** by Peggy Gaddis
  Two men came into Jill Barclay's lonely life—one to bring happiness and the other to destroy it.
  #92-634, 50¢

- [ ] **BEYOND THE CLOUDS,** by Delphina McCarthy
  Pretty Pat Aylmer found excitement in international flying—and disappointment in shattered dreams.
  #92-635, 50¢

- [ ] **PEACOCK HILL,** by Peggy Gaddis
  The story of a young woman who became a widow one hour after her marriage and the strange secret which haunted her.
  #B50-637, 50¢

- [ ] **THE LOVING HEART,** by Joan Garrison
  Lovely Doris Scott was captured—and enraptured—by a double involvement.
  #B50-638, 50¢

- [ ] **THE PERSISTENT SUITOR,** by Peggy Gaddis
  The Bentley sisters came to their secluded island paradise to forget their bitter disappointments in love. *But they were not alone.*
  #B50-649, 50¢

- [ ] **ESCAPE FROM LOVE,** by Betty Blocklinger
  The tender story of a woman who was unable to face love until she had the chance to escape from it.
  #B50-650, 50¢

- [ ] **NURSE BY NIGHT,** by Doris Knight
  A nurse in love with a doctor is not unusual, but Norma and Tony were unusual people . . .
  #B45-902, 45¢

- [ ] **THE JOYOUS HILLS,** by Peggy Gaddis
  A big city career girl seeks solitude in the Joyous Hills, but finds something else . . .
  #B50-653, 50¢

- [ ] **SNATCH A DREAM,** by Joan Garrison
  Life holds such a great promise . . . but Mary felt trapped in a small town, forced to run a small business.
  #B50-654, 50¢

- [ ] **WAIT FOR THE DAY,** by Marguerite Nelson
  She was engaged to Brad, but she knew she was losing him . . . slowly but inevitably.
  #B50-658, 50¢

- [ ] **BELOVED INTRUDER,** by Peggy Gaddis
  Joyce Hilliard was a New York girl in love with an Atlanta man, but when she went to Atlanta to marry him she found herself an intruder in what would be her own home.
  #B50-659, 50¢

- [ ] **COME INTO MY HEART,** by Peggy Gaddis
  A practical joke catapulted Kerry Martens into a deep conflict—which of the two Waterman brothers could she really be happy with?
  #B50-665, 50¢

- [ ] **READY TO LOVE,** by Jeanne Bowman
  She had been too busy for love—now she feared love was not ready for *her.*
  #B50-666, 50¢

- [ ] **A LITTLE LOVE,** by Peggy Gaddis
  The wedding plans were made, but Kelcy's bridegroom eloped with the maid of honor . . .
  #B50-671, 50¢

- [ ] **CLOVER HILL,** by Ethel Bangert
  A four-sided triangle brought complications too difficult for young Julie Bond.
  #B50-672, 50¢

- [ ] **HOMECOMING,** by Adeline McElfresh
  Ann Merick returned from her vacation to find her best friend married to her sweetheart.
  #B50-660, 50¢

- [ ] **WHERE LOVE IS,** by Peggy Gaddis
  A carefree young woman is forced to decide between the two men who love her.
  #B50-661, 50¢

- [ ] **REHEARSAL FOR A WEDDING,** by Peggy Gaddis
  She was determined to achieve security, even if it meant stealing her best friend's childhood sweetheart.
  #B50-673, 50¢

- [ ] **A TIME FOR STRENGTH,** Nell Marr Dean
  Dr. Janice Stanford was at the crossroads of the most important decision of her young life.
  #B50-677, 50¢

☐ **ROBIN**, Peggy Gaddis
The girl was young, attractive and ready for life—but romance was to be denied her. #B50-678, 50¢

☐ **GOLDEN RAIN**, Irene Roberts
All was bleak and hopeless until a charming young playwright walked into Carol's life. #B50-679, 50¢

☐ **SHATTERED HALO**, by Adeline McElfresh
A young woman's certainty about love—and life—was shattered by a series of anonymous telephone calls. #B50-674, 50¢

☐ **WEDDING SONG**, Peggy Gaddis
Through the veil of overburdening problems Nora sees a new life, a new love—and a new enchantment. #B50-684, 50¢

☐ **THE QUESTING HEART**, Joan Garrison
Little did she dream that her devotion to duty would place in jeopardy her devotion to the man she loved. #B50-685, 50¢

Romantic Suspense Novels

☐ **HOUSE OF MIST**, by Maria Luisa Bombal
Evil menace and fatal suspicion lurk in the mansion where the dark shadow of a young girl's dreams become dread reality. #92-610, 50¢

☐ **THE STARVED**, by Arthur Thompson
An extraordinary novel of a woman born in sorrow, in love with a man she doesn't know. #92-616, 50¢

☐ **MIRROR OF DELUSION**, by Mary Reisner
Her name was Charlotte; she walked in mystery, lived for love, and feared the inevitable tragedy. "Captivating"—*New York Times*. #93-051, 60¢

☐ **DOORS TO DEATH**, by Lee Crosby
What was the mystery of Crane Mansion? A secret so horrible that neither love nor death could reveal it. #B50-629, 50¢

☐ **SHADOWS ON THE WALL**, by Mary Reisner
Death visited the huge Victorian house, perhaps he had come to stay . . .
#B50-641, 50¢

☐ **THE SECRET OF KENSINGTON MANOR**, by Genevieve St. John
Why did Lori Kensington have to come here to die? Or was it to find love . . . ?
#B60-053, 60¢

☐ **BRIDGE HOUSE**, by Lee Crosby
Would love be enough? Could a woman's faith and trust unlock the terrible secret of Bridge House? #B50-644, 50¢

☐ **HOUSE OF COBWEBS**, by Mary Reisner
The House of Cobwebs is a trap spun maliciously for Serena and the man she loved. Could they escape with their lives—and their love? #B60-052, 60¢

☐ **HOUSE OF DISTANT VOICES**, by Evelyn Bond
How could anyone know what she was going through, when she herself wasn't certain? #B50-662, 50¢

☐ **THE DARK WATCH**, by Genevieve St. John
She was proud and proper—but she loved a man with a fierce temper.
#B50-667, 50¢

☐ **THE SHADOW ON SPANISH SWAMP**, by Genevieve St. John
She had been warned, but she refused to believe she was a bride of Death.
#B50-669, 50¢

☐ **THE VICTORIAN CROWN**, by Edwina Noone
Her only hope for romance—or even life—lay in The Victorian Crown.
#B50-675, 50¢

☐ **THE HOUSE ON CABRA**, June Wetherell
She shuddered in fear from every footstep, for danger—even violent death—lurked in every corner of the old Bath House. #B50-681, 50¢